G000146959

Never be Lonely

By the same author

Reluctant for Romance

Romantic Melody

Widow On The World

High Infidelity

A Blessing in Disguise

Second Best

A Change for the Better

Never be Lonely

Pamela Fudge

ROBERT HALE · LONDON

First published in Great Britain 2011

ISBN 978-0-7090-9253-7

Robert Hale Limited
Clerkenwell House
Clerkenwell Green
London EC1R 0HT

www.halebooks.com

2 4 6 8 10 9 7 5 3 1

Typeset in 11/17pt New Century Schoolbook
Printed in Great Britain by the UK by the
MPG Books Group, Bodmin and King's Lynn

This book is dedicated to colleagues who became dear friends in the HSC Admissions Office at Bournemouth University, like Pam M, Kate H, Sarah, Kate T, Jill, Jane, Gail, Angela, Alison, Katrina, Michelle and to the brilliant Midwifery Team. The years I have worked with you all have been a pleasure.

ACKNOWLEDGEMENTS

My thanks go to all at Robert Hale Ltd, especially John Hale, Paola Motka, Gill Jackson, Nick Chaytor, Catherine Williams and David Young.

Having only ever seen Canada from a visitor's point of view, I owe grateful thanks to my sister, Barb Porpaczy, who patiently answered my many questions about life in British Columbia. Also to my niece, Laura Nicholls, who did the same, and with her sons, Henry and Matthew, took photographs of numerous churches so that I could make an accurate description of the one I chose to use in this book. (Nice work, guys!) In addition I want to thank my friend and colleague, Kate Hearn, for her detailed advice regarding the recruitment process for applicants wanting to train as Social Workers.

I am so lucky to have wonderful friends – fellow writers, like Pam W, Chris H, Nora, Lyndsay, Alan, Bruna, Ann, Rob R, Cass and Janie, and those I relax with, including Karen, Chris N, Jan, Nicky, Sally, Robert M and Robert B. Not forgetting my stepdaughters, Rachel and Debbie, my webmaster and stepson, Mark, my sister, Pat, and my gorgeous grandchildren, Abbie, Emma, Tyler and Bailey.

Most of all, my love and thanks go to my children, Shane, Kelly, Scott, and not forgetting Mike and Jess. I am blessed to have your love and support. www.pamfudge.co.uk

1

I had been to any number of funerals in my forty-three years. They increasingly become a fact of life as you and everyone around you grows older, but this one had to be the strangest by far.

On this occasion I didn't know a living soul among the mourners and barely remembered the deceased – a man who was little more than a vague memory of someone I'd known briefly as a child. Now I was here I couldn't understand what fanciful whim had brought me all this way to pay my respects to someone who certainly wasn't worthy of my respect.

The oddness of the situation wasn't helped by the fact that here in Canada such occasions were evidently more along the lines of a memorial service. I'd thought those were only for the rich and famous and Mitchell Browning was neither.

The chain of events that had brought me here had started out of the blue with a phone call, the line so clear I had no way of knowing it was an international one.

'Is that Francesca Dudley?' A female voice I hadn't recognized asked the question, very abruptly, the minute I'd answered the phone with my usual brief, 'Hello'. Then she continued as soon as I acquiesced, 'Well, you won't know me, but I thought you should know Mitchell Browning has passed away. The service in his memory is on Thursday of next week. Perhaps you might like to attend?'

Shocked that he was alive, and then shocked that he was dead, I immediately decided I wouldn't go. After all, what would be the point? Then, quite illogically I changed my mind and decided that I would attend – out of curiosity if nothing else.

'Where will the service be held?'

That was how I found myself attending a memorial service for my father in a church that was strange to me, yet oddly reminiscent of those at home thousands of miles away in England with similar stone walls and high arched windows. From the time I'd walked out of my own front door and climbed into the taxi taking me to the airport, the thought uppermost in my mind was that this would be similar to the journey that he had made and in making it he could hardly have put a greater distance between us if he had tried.

I arrived at my destination jet-lagged, dazed and disorientated after a nine and-a-half hour flight from Gatwick to Vancouver, followed swiftly by a connecting flight across to Vancouver Island. Met at Victoria Airport by a total stranger it felt like no time at all before I found myself attending a service in celebration of my estranged father's life. I had barely made it, and now that I had all the effort made to get there in time seemed rather pointless. I wasn't at all sure what I – or anyone else for that matter – thought my presence would achieve.

Dressed in a sadly creased grey trouser suit, aware that my dark hair was messily escaping from its tortoiseshell clip, I stood calm and silent amid the smartly dressed mourners, unmoved by the solemnity of the service and the ready tears of those standing around me. I could only dredge up a little reluctant sadness that if there *had* to be a reunion after so many years apart we couldn't both have been there to see it.

I didn't recognize Mitchell Browning from the large coloured photograph of a smiling, grey-haired man that stood in pride of place at the front of the church. Neither did I recognize the individual the minister began describing in glowing terms, such as upstanding citizen, caring neighbour, etcetera, etcetera, etcetera, so very soon I tuned out and dug deep into my mind and way, way back until I found the person I did recognize.

Mitchell Browning, my father, had been as dark haired as me in those far off days when he was still part of my life. He was clean-shaven in what was obviously a very recent photograph, but when I'd known him he'd sported the distinctive drooping moustache that men appeared to favour in the seventies if the old television programmes and well-known singers of the day were anything to go by. I had inherited the curly hair that suited him, but remained the bane of my life and made me thank God every day for the invention of the straightening irons and lotions that tamed the tangles without too much effort.

I'd have been no more than four years old when my father walked out of my life yet I found, now that I was making the effort, I could still clearly picture a tall man, lean to the point of skinny, wearing the colourful big-collared shirts and flared trousers that were also in fashion. I'd seen enough pictures since of that era to know he was typical of his generation and he'd probably even worn the Brut aftershave Henry Cooper encouraged men to 'splash all over'. I thought I would have recognized the scent of him anywhere – even after all these years.

If I tried very hard, I could just grasp memories of walking to the paper shop on a Sunday morning and being carried home and up the stairs to our flat high on my father's shoulders with a pocketful of sweeties. Without fail he'd be told sternly by my mother, 'You're wasting money we can't afford and ruining that child's appetite *and* her teeth'. His wink behind her back had always helped to take the sting from her words.

Most nights he'd be the one to tuck me up in bed, reading me stories and taking on the voices of each character so that the world of make-believe came alive for me. I supposed I had him to thank for the love of books that had never left me and even after all these years the lives of fictional characters often seemed infinitely preferable to my own far more humdrum existence. I'd accepted long ago that fairy-tale endings weren't for the likes of me.

The organ striking up shocked me back to the present and into a scenario as fantastic as any fictional plot. What on earth had I been thinking of to fly halfway round the world to pay my last respects to someone who clearly had no regard at all for me – his own child?

Who were these people? And why had my father chosen to share his life with them rather than the wife and daughter he had left behind, seemingly without a thought, and certainly without any intention of keeping in touch?

I shouldn't have come. I knew that now. It had been a huge mistake on my part. My mother often pointed out that I was inclined to act without thinking of the consequences, and on this occasion she was definitely right. What she was going to have to say about me coming here I dreaded to think, but then I'd always had the feeling that she had never quite understood the huge gap my father leaving had left in my life, or the desperate need I had carried deep inside to know why he had done it.

The minister was speaking again and his words washed over me, until two words leapt out from the rest: 'Family man.'

It was all I could do to remain seated and not to jump up and voice a protest – to point out that Mitchell Browning was anything *but* a family man. I should have known, been prepared, but the pain was indescribable as I was forced to face the fact that he had turned his back on me, his first-born, only to move away and start another family without a second thought – and without wasting a moment, if the man presently making his way to the front of the church was his son.

Tall and dark, dressed in a sombre suit and tie – and clearly of a similar age to me – the man's face was grave but as he began to speak it broke into a smile.

'What can I say about Mitch?' he said, his voice deep and as smooth as dark chocolate. 'He was the father I never really knew.'

Eh? Pardon? Wasn't that my line? I subsided against the back of the seat, totally confused and waited for him to go on.

'Most of you know, right, that Mitch married my mother when he was in his thirties and I was already in my teens. My own father had died when I was quite young, you know, but the few memories I had of him were special and, if I was honest, I didn't want anyone trying to take his place. Without me ever telling Mitch this, he assured me that he accepted I would only ever have one father but he hoped he could be my friend. I just wanted to say today that he was the best friend I ever had and I will miss him more than words can say.'

I felt a mixture of emotions. In spite of myself, I was touched by the sincerity of his words, curiously relieved, but also filled with bitter fury that the only father I would ever have could turn his back on me and then go on to create a loving relationship with a child that wasn't even his own flesh and blood.

I watched the tall man go back to his seat, and hug a woman who could only be his mother – and Mitchell Browning's wife. Solidly built, with blonde hair, she was so like the woman who had collected me from the airport that there could be no doubting they were sisters.

We had exchanged little more than pleasantries since I'd arrived on Canadian soil, but I guessed Julie Sowerby had been the one to inform me of my father's death. She had taken care of all my travel arrangements and insisted I would be staying in her home as a welcome guest. On our arrival at the church, she had been clearly unhappy at my insistence on going to sit near the back of the church so that I could blend in with the other mourners. In the end she'd accepted she had no choice but to leave me in order to offer support to her sister sitting at the front. I wondered if she was the only one who knew who I was and what I was doing there.

I could see Julie now, moving in to comfort her sister, and I watched as the son offered his mother a handkerchief from his suit pocket. I felt very alone and wondered again why I had come when I clearly didn't belong and couldn't even share in their very obvious grief and loss.

As I watched a blonde girl came into view and the stepson put his other arm around her, drawing her close into the family group. Probably his girlfriend, I surmised idly. She was very pretty, though a bit young for a man of his age I would have thought, since she looked no more than seventeen or eighteen years old. She was clearly upset and weeping bitterly and Mitchell Browning's widow used the handkerchief she was still holding to dry the girl's tears tenderly.

They were hidden from view then as everyone rose to sing another hymn. I would slip away after this, I decided, before the service came to an end. I didn't want to be caught up in the surge of mourners and perhaps have to face unwelcome questions, and the last thing – the very *last* thing I wanted was to meet the immediate family. I could wait unobtrusively outside until Julie came to find me.

I was reaching for my handbag and preparing to leave as the hymn came to an end, hoping not to be noticed in the flurry of everyone closing songbooks and taking seats. I had already taken a step towards the aisle when my attention was caught by a movement at the front of the church and, even as I turned to see what was happening, I realized I had missed the chance to leave unobtrusively.

The blonde girl had stepped away from the family and into the aisle. Dressed from head to toe in black, she looked small and very fragile, but walked forward with steely determination evident in the straightness of her back and the rigid set of her shoulders.

The tall guy went after her, and in the silence he could be clearly heard as he pleaded, 'You don't have to do this, Ashlyn'.

She turned to look up at him and said firmly, 'Oh, yes, Jared, I do'.

Reaching the lectern she scrabbled in her bag until she found the crumpled piece of paper she'd obviously been searching for, spread it out carefully in front of her and then without so much as glancing at it, she began to speak.

'Mitchell Browning,' she said, without hesitation or a single tremor in her clear tone, 'was a wonderful man.'

I could feel my eyebrows lift almost to meet my hairline and wondered what gave her the right or the knowledge to speak about my father in such a way.

'He was,' she continued, interrupting my sceptical line of thought, 'a good friend and neighbour, as most of you here will gladly testify, right?'

There was a murmur of assent, an eager nodding of heads throughout the congregation.

'He would,' she went on, 'do anything for anybody and knew the true meaning of the community spirit and,' she paused for effect, 'the true meaning of family. The many children he took under his wing will tell you he was the best foster father in the world. Jared used the word friend instead of father, but in his case – as his stepfather – it meant the same thing. They are all absolutely right, you know, he was the best father in the whole world. I know that better than anyone, because Mitchell Browning was my beloved dad.'

2

I gasped audibly. The shock of the girl's sentimental words almost took my legs out from under me and I reached out to grasp the back of the seat in front of me before slumping onto the seat behind.

I almost laughed out loud as I realized I had allowed myself to be lulled into a false sense of security. Without acknowledging it even to myself, I had always foolishly allowed myself to believe that I was Mitchell Browning's only natural child. I knew better now. It might have taken him a good few years but in the end he had really done it – created another daughter to take the place of the one he had discarded without a thought.

I knew I couldn't stay and listen in silence for another minute to tributes honestly paid but meaningless to me. As soon as the music began again I stumbled to the door, heedless of the heads turning and the curious stares, and out into the sunlight beyond.

Taking deep steadying breaths, I walked, blinking hard to clear the tears I resolutely refused to shed over someone who had had so little regard for my feelings or for me. I was merely the child Mitchell Browning had thoughtlessly spawned and then, equally thoughtlessly, discarded and forgotten all about when he grew tired of family life.

I walked and walked, through wide and unfamiliar streets, almost getting mown down when I stepped off what was called the sidewalk here and into the path of a car because I'd forgotten everyone drove on the other side of the road in Canada. The blare of the horn brought me to my senses. I stepped back hastily, staring through the windscreen at the furious gestures and silently mouthed obscenities of the male driver who was probably more shocked than angry.

What on earth had possessed me to travel all those thousands of miles? It was probably one of the most pointless things I had done in my entire life. In any other circumstance I would have been thrilled to find myself in Canada but at that precise moment the wonders of what was probably a beautiful country were lost on me. All I could think of was getting the first available flight home and putting this whole sorry experience behind me. I felt sure it could be arranged; all I had to do was make it clear to the kindly Julie that, for me, coming here had been a big mistake.

Feeling much better once the decision had been made, I stopped and looked around me. It was only then I realized that after mindlessly walking for so long I had no idea of where exactly I was or, indeed, where I might be going. To my utter horror, I also realized, far too late, that in my haste to get away I had dropped my handbag with all my cards and money, my passport, Julie Sowerby's contact details and, more importantly, my return air tickets, probably back there in the church.

It was difficult not to panic, but I forced myself to stand absolutely still and try to get my bearings. I couldn't have come very far, could I? How long had I been walking. Surely not that long: All I had to do was to retrace my steps.

It seemed to take forever but, at last, I thought the road I turned into seemed familiar and, sure enough, there was the church, tall and majestic right in front of me. With its grey stone walls and leaded windows it really could have been any church in England and I wished with all my wounded heart that it was.

The place was deserted, of course, the door I had left by was locked and, right on cue large drops of rain began to fall from a sky turned suddenly overcast.

For a moment I stood helplessly undecided, and was quickly soaked in my suit jacket and trousers. Then I ran as close as I could to the side of the building until I found another door – unlocked this time – at the back. I let myself in.

It was dark inside, just a little light came through the narrow windows, but it was calm and peaceful and just what I needed at that moment – along with time. Time to sit and accept that the dream – the one I had only just realized I'd been carrying with me for most of my life – was never going to come true. The precious dream that the father I had never, ever forgotten or stopped loving was going to come looking for me.

Grief such as I had never known swamped me. It filled my head, my heart, my whole body and I howled my hurt to the rafters, screaming, '*Why?*' to someone who could not answer me even had he wanted to.

The storm outside was nothing to the storm within me, but eventually both subsided. I rubbed my face with a tissue I found tucked in my pocket and then I sat calmly and wondered what I was going to do. There was no sign of my handbag – I hadn't really expected there to be.

Eventually I made my way back outside and, feeling more tired than I had ever felt in my life, I walked slowly to the front of the building.

'Oh, there you are,' said a feminine voice filled with relief, and there coming towards me was Julie Sowerby, followed closely by Jared whatever-his-name-was. 'We thought you were lost in the wilds of Victoria, right, Jared?'

'Something like that,' from his tone it was very evident he, at least, had wished me permanently lost.

'I'm so sorry.' I felt obliged to apologize to Julie, who had clearly been worried, if not to this frowning man who obviously had not.

'Don't be,' she urged kindly, 'you probably found this all very upsetting, which is quite understandable, you know. Look, I have your purse.' She held out my handbag to me.

'Shall we get going before it starts to rain again?' Jared sounded faintly bored, and he was looking me up and down as if I were no more than a nuisance, someone akin to an annoying and disobedient child who had wandered off and become lost. 'Mom will wonder where we've got to.'

Oh, God, they weren't taking me back to the wake, or whatever they called such occasions in this country, were they? I cringed at the thought.

I suspected Julie saw the panic stricken look on my face and had interpreted it correctly when she said, 'You look very tired, Francesca. Would you prefer to go straight back to my house?'

I nodded gratefully. 'Would you mind?'

'Perhaps we could all make up our minds and get going,' Jared said tersely, ushering us in the general direction of a huge four by four vehicle parked beside the road. I'd noticed such vehicles seemed to be prevalent here, unlike in England where all but celebrities and the very rich were being persuaded to go green or were downsizing in order to economize.

Without waiting to be invited, I climbed into the backseat, ignoring the front passenger door that Jared held open, quite obviously for me, with a belated show of manners. He might have looked foolish – something else he could have disliked me for, because he evidently had something against me – if Julie hadn't slipped into the front seat instead.

'We're going to my place, Jared,' Julie told him as he pulled away from the curb, flicking the windscreen wipers on as the rain began to fall again, making me wonder if this particular part of Canada was always as wet as this in May.

'But Mum will be looking for you, Aunt Julie. She needs you, especially today, you know.'

If he was trying to make me feel uncomfortable, Jared was doing a good job. Obviously, his newly widowed mother was going to need the support of her sister today of all days and here I was taking her away from her family.

Before I could reluctantly relent and say I would go with them, Julie thankfully took control, saying easily, 'Just drop us off and go back to your Mum. I will follow as soon as I get Francesca settled. I won't be too long.'

'But we left your car at Mum's.'

'I can take a cab. It's no trouble at all.'

I could tell by the way Jared clenched his jaw that the arrangement didn't please him. I wondered if anything did – but then reminded myself that he *had* recently lost his stepfather. Close behind that came the thought that he might try remembering that I'd just lost my father and that it was the second time around for me *and*, unlike him, I had precious few memories of the time I'd shared with him to comfort me.

It seemed no time at all before we swept into the curved driveway of a rather grand house that had apparently been built into the solid rock of a Canadian hillside. Wisteria in bloom climbed up to the wooden veranda that ran around the first floor, its gnarled trunk easily as thick as my wrist, the delicate blooms drooping all over to create a beautiful mist of blue.

Jared drove off the minute we were out of his monstrous car, the furious roar of the engine showing his displeasure.

'He's not usually so short tempered, you know,' Julie excused her nephew, and then she put her hand up to her face and exclaimed, 'Your luggage – it's still in the trunk of my car.'

I struggled to hide my disappointment, feeling I had caused enough trouble for one day. 'Don't worry, I can easily sleep in my underwear.'

Julie laughed then. 'Oh, I think we can do better than that,' she said, and urged me up the steep stone steps to the front door – or should I say doors, since there were two – and in minutes we were inside a tiled vestibule.

Despite my fatigue I found myself looking around curiously.

There was a closet to the right, presumably for shoes and coats, and I caught sight of some sort of sitting room to the left. Julie pointed to a closed door ahead and said, 'The laundry room,' and ushering me around the corner, indicated right, 'my office,' left, 'your bathroom' and going ahead at the end of the corridor, she threw open a door and said, 'This will be your room for as long as you care to stay, right? Please make yourself at home, Francesca, you are very welcome here.'

'You're very kind,' I said, taking in a sizeable room that ran from the front of the house to the back and which, despite its ample proportions, was dominated by the huge bed centred against the back wall. Looking at it longingly all I could think of was crawling under the covers and losing myself – and my troubled thoughts – in sleep.

'There are towels already in the bathroom and I'll bring you one of my nightdresses. Now can I get you anything to eat? You must be hungry.'

'No, really,' I was horrified at the thought of putting the kindly woman to any more trouble. 'I'm just desperately in need of a shower and bed.'

'Well, my home is yours, my dear.'

I couldn't help it, I had to ask, 'Why did you ask me to come and why are you being so kind to me?'

She smiled, her eyes crinkling in a face with scarcely more than laughter lines, despite the fact she must be at least fifteen to twenty years older than me. 'You're family,' she said.

'Hardly.' The word came out more abruptly than I'd intended, but Julie had already turned away and didn't seem to have heard me.

I took my time in the bathroom, showering and washing my hair and making full use of the impressive array of toiletries. There was even a brand new toothbrush and I felt like a brand new person when I finally emerged enfolded in the soft towelling robe I'd found hanging behind the door. I had every intention of effusively thanking my hostess for her generous hospitality and blaming my previous cranky attitude on jet lag.

However, Julie had obviously gone back to be with her sister, leaving a note in my room urging me to make myself at home and supper on a tray. I was very hungry and the poached salmon, new potatoes and salad were delicious, but I had taken no more than a few mouthfuls before exhaustion got the better of me. Pulling on the plain cotton nightdress folded in readiness on the bed I climbed thankfully under the covers and was asleep in seconds.

There were venetian blinds across the wide windows at the far end of the room but I hadn't thought to close the slats and woke to sunshine pouring in and birds singing outside. Reluctant to surface just yet, I burrowed more deeply under the covers and wished the birds to kingdom come.

A tentative tap on the door made me resurface but, before I could speak, Julie's fair head and smiling face appeared.

'Oh, you are awake.' She came right in bearing a loaded tray. 'Did you sleep well?'

'Mmm, I did, thank you, but you didn't have to bring me breakfast in bed – really you didn't.'

'Nonsense. It's no trouble at all and it's nice to have someone else in the house for once, apart from Kizzy,' she nodded at the black and white cat who had followed her into the room, jumped onto the bed, and was now making herself comfortable at the foot of it.

'What time is it?' I asked, as the tray was settled on my knees and I was able to view grapefruit segments in a dish, scrambled egg on toast, not to mention a little pot of tea. 'This looks delicious, thank you.'

'It's about eleven thirty.'

'*Eleven thirty*?' I gasped and tried to push the tray away. 'Whatever must you think of me? I never sleep past seven at home.'

Julie hurried forward and pressed me, quite firmly, back against the pillows and straightened the tray. 'You were exhausted,' she pointed out. 'Now, if you go to bed tonight at your normal time – our time – you will be right as ninepence tomorrow. Just take your time this morning, because there really is no hurry.'

'But what about your sister?' I fretted, 'I shouldn't be taking you away from her. She needs you.'

'Cheryl has her children.'

'Does she – does she know who I am and that I'm here?'

'Yes, she does. It was she who asked me to ring you. She would like to meet you, when you feel up to it. Now,' Julie became brusque, 'eat up. Your luggage is over there – I would have unpacked it if I hadn't thought I would disturb you. When you're ready – and there is no rush at all – come on upstairs and we can make plans for what's left of the day.'

Picking up last night's tray with its wasted food, she called the cat and they both left, leaving me to enjoy my breakfast.

As I ate I looked around me with far more interest than I had shown the night before.

Fitted closets ran almost the length of one wall, with a big solid chest of drawers on the opposite side of a room so vast there was still space at the window end for a chaise longue, a comfortable armchair, a round table with fresh flowers on it and even a writing desk with an upright chair, without the room feeling the least bit crowded.

During my perusal of what was obviously the guest bedroom I had been steadily working my way through the contents of the tray until, finally replete, I pushed it away and threw back the covers, ready to face what was left of the day. It was only then I realized I hadn't shared my intention to return home immediately with Julie.

Taking my cue from Julie I dressed in jeans and a white T-shirt and carrying a light knitted jacket, I went to find her. The house was split-level and would have been quite unusual in England. It was certainly spacious and as I mounted the stairs I could see through the banister rails on either side a charming sitting room to the left and a dining room on my right. It was all furnished in a very English manner with polished mahogany furniture and loose covers on the sofas.

Following the chink of china and the sound of cupboard doors opening and closing I found myself in a light and airy kitchen with enough room for a round table and four chairs at one end.

Julie turned to face me and said with a pleased smile, 'Oh, you're looking much better, you know. Here, let me take the tray. Can I make tea for you or would you prefer coffee?'

'Whatever you're having would be great,' I found myself smiling back and wondered how I was going to broach the matter of my leaving sooner than later without seeming extremely ungrateful.

'I'll make tea,' she decided, reaching to take a teapot down from a white dresser at the dining end of the kitchen. All the kitchen units were white, as were the table and chairs and a small, upholstered armchair set close by the bay window with an open paperback on its seat. The book was by Anita Shreve, I noticed, and it was one I had read myself.

'Mitch gave us all a taste for tea,' Julie was saying as she carried the tray over to the table and set it down. 'Sugar and milk?' she asked and then, she looked at me. 'Do you mind me talking about Mitch – your father – or does it upset you?'

I shrugged. 'Why should it? After all, I barely knew the man. I have no idea why I came all this way to pay my respects to a man I scarcely remember – or why you invited me, for that matter.'

'I – we thought it was something you might regret if you didn't get the opportunity.'

'I would have thought all of the regrets might have been his. I had no control over our relationship – or the lack of one – since I was just a small child when my father left and was given no choice over what happened between my parents, or even an explanation.' I knew I sounded bitter, but felt I was entitled to feel that way and so I didn't try to hide it. I changed the subject abruptly. 'This is a beautiful house. Do you live here alone?'

Julie grinned ruefully, 'Just me and the cat rattling around in all these rooms since the husband traded me in for a younger model and my grown-up children departed for the bright lights of Vancouver. I'm loathe to leave the garden,' she added by way of explanation and with a nod towards the window.

'Mmm, I can see why,' I said, taking in the lush lawns, trees and shrubs, and the brilliant colours of the daffodils, pansies and tulips filling the borders. 'A lot of work, though, I should imagine.'

'I have help with the heavy work, outside and in,' Julie poured the tea into delicate bone china cups.

'I've never seen so many birds.' I turned back again to the window. 'I recognize most of them, but what on earth are those tiny ones?'

'Oh, those are hummingbirds. Don't you have those in England?'

'No.' I shook my head, fascinated by the bird I could see hovering around some sort of feeder, dipping its long thin beak in to sip the liquid inside, the wings were never more than a blur.

I turned reluctantly back to the table, and lifting the cup in front of me took a sip of a surprisingly good cup of tea.

'I thought,' Julie was saying, 'that we could go to downtown Victoria. You should see more of the place than the airport and a couple of streets in the suburbs. We can shop, if you like, you might like to send postcards to your friends.'

'Hardly anyone knows I'm here.' I didn't add that I rarely mentioned my father. I could never think of anything to say. I wasn't exactly proud of the fact that he'd abandoned me. 'Thank you, though,' I remembered my manners, 'it would be nice to see something of Victoria now that I'm here.' So much for making my desire for an early departure clear, I thought wryly, but then I would be the first to admit that assertiveness never had been my strong point.

Julie insisted on taking photos of me around the town – just as if I was a regular tourist. One outside of a shop captured me standing beside an enormous stuffed bear dressed in the familiar red coat of the mounted police Canada was famous for, and another with a stuffed moose a bit further along the street. She pointed out the imposing parliament building in the distance and promised we would make our way down there some other time and perhaps take tea at the Empress Hotel nearby.

We looked at touristy things, T-shirts, miniature totem poles and guidebooks. I resisted them all until I found a pair of hummingbird earrings in silver and knew I must have them, even if I never purchased another thing.

The day was sunny and surprisingly warm and as we turned into a side street I could see a glimpse of the sea at the bottom of the hill.

'The harbour,' Julie indicated. 'I thought we might enjoy a late lunch outside, and watch the flying boats land and take off.'

I didn't think I'd be able to eat another thing after my hearty breakfast, but the paninis were delicious and I was charmed to find the shape of a maple leaf in the creamy froth on my cup of latte.

'Do you have family?' Julie asked, adding awkwardly, 'Well, apart from Mitch, of course. Your mother is still alive, right? Any brothers or sisters?'

'My mother is still alive and lives with my stepfather, usually for several months of each year in Spain. Like you I have an ex-husband and I live on my own with my cat. I have no other family apart from the sister I never knew existed right here in Canada.'

'I think it's time the two of you met,' Julie said in a firm tone that brooked no argument and, gathering up her handbag, she made her way back up the hill, leaving me no choice but to follow her on extremely reluctant feet.

Throughout a rather lonely childhood I had wished for a sister – almost as hard as I had wished for my father to come home. I could have accepted a half-sister from my mother and stepfather's relationship without any problem. What I couldn't accept was the sibling who'd had my father's love for the whole of her growing up – the very thing I had been denied. I didn't care that it was illogical and I was a grown woman who should have known better, I was prepared to hate her on sight.

3

We drew up in front of a two-storey house, the garden neatly planted with spring flowers. Tall tulips lined the winding path that would take us to the front door. I noted it all, but the attractive exterior was wasted on me as I wished myself anywhere else in the world but where I was. I felt quite sick.

As Julie turned off the engine, I placed my hand on her arm. 'Are you sure this is a good idea?' I asked nervously.

'I think this meeting is long overdue,' she said firmly, and stepped from the car leaving me little choice but to do the same, wondering as I followed Julie why I had ever left England and put myself at the mercy of this family of strangers.

Without bothering to ring the doorbell, Julie let herself into a neat hallway and announced, 'We're here,' in a way that made me wonder if we were expected.

Three people arrived from three different directions, wearing three very different expressions: Cheryl came from what was obviously the kitchen wiping her hands on a tea towel and looking slightly anxious; Jared came in from the garden at the back of the house wearing the frown I was already accustomed to seeing on his face each time we met; the girl, Ashlyn, came hurtling in from another room, all tousled blonde hair and endless legs, skidded to a halt right in front of me and almost blinded me with the brilliance of a smile so wide and joyful it completely took me by surprise.

'You're *here*,' she said breathlessly. 'You're really here. I can hardly believe it. I've wanted a sister of my own for all of my life.'

I was lost for words, but that didn't seem to matter. In fact, I doubt anyone really noticed since Ashlyn more than made up for my silence.

'We look really alike, right?' she demanded, coming to stand close by my side. 'I think we do, you know.'

Three people contemplated any similarities – real or imagined – between us.

'Actually, you could be taken for si – sisters,' Cheryl stumbled over the word, as she realized what she was saying and then added quickly, 'which, of course, you are.'

'There is a definite likeness – despite the very dark and very fair hair.' This came from Julie.

'Oh,' Ashlyn pleaded, fixing me with her blue gaze, 'please tell me you have the frizzy hair, too.' She reached out to touch a loose tendril by my ear, and it was all I could do not to flinch away, totally unused to such familiarity. 'It would just be so unfair if it was only me who has to spend hours using lotions and ceramic straighteners.'

'I have it, too,' I said dryly, struggling to accept I really was having this bizarre conversation with a sibling I hadn't known existed until the day before.

Cheryl suddenly seemed to remember her manners and insisted on making tea, urging me to sit down and make myself at home. I sat and looked around a charming room, cosily furnished, but cluttered with family photos that took up every available surface and hung from the walls, too. There were different groups of children surrounding my father and his wife in every one. Looking at those pictures it seemed painfully obvious he'd been prepared to welcome every child he'd ever come across into his life and home – apart from me. That hurt, it really hurt.

I was furious but fascinated, too, and found it hard to stop myself swivelling my head this way and that. I might have given in to the urge had it not been for Jared's brooding presence. He, alone, made no pretence of being pleased to have me there, and I knew he would have been just as pleased to see me leave as I would have been to go.

I could have been anybody sitting in that house. In truth I was an interloper – a nobody – a nobody in this country and in this house; a nobody surrounded by photos of my dead father's real family of step, natural and fostered children. It was clear that besides the replacement daughter he had eventually sired, Mitchell Browning had spent his life fathering other people's children yet had apparently never given a second thought to the child he had left in England crying for him and wondering what she could have done that was so terrible it had made him leave.

Once the bustle of bringing in tea trays and plates of what looked suspiciously like home-baked cakes and pastries was over, we sat nursing our cups and saucers and an uncomfortable silence settled over us. There was nothing I could think of to say to break it, but Ashlyn, not unexpectedly, had no such reservations.

'Weren't you ever curious about us?' she asked suddenly and very bluntly. 'Didn't you ever want to come across and meet us?'

I stared at her, and then I shrugged in what I hoped was a suitably uncaring manner. 'Why would I when I had absolutely no idea any of you even existed? I never knew where he – Mitchell Browning – went when he left me – us. I was four years old then, and I never heard his name mentioned again until Julie phoned last week to tell me he had died.'

There was a collective gasp – even Jared sat up and took notice finally, shock replacing the disapproving look that had been on his face ever since I had stepped into the family home.

It was Julie who spoke, as, nodding, she said, 'I don't know why I'm surprised because somehow I thought that might be the case.'

'I don't know why you're surprised either, any of you. You must know he died neither knowing nor caring what had become of me. Why would he?' I queried bitterly indicating the photographs around the room. 'He obviously wasted no time creating a brand new family as far away from his original one as he could get.'

'No, that's not true,' Cheryl insisted hotly, 'he never forgot you, not ever, not even for a minute.'

'Then why didn't he have any contact with us? Tell me that.' My voice was flat, matter-of-fact, even uncaring, but I was dismayed to detect a slight tremor in my tone. I only hoped no one else had noticed.

'But he did.'

I glared at Cheryl. 'I can assure you he did *not*. There has been no contact between my father and me – and I use the title loosely since he was no father to me – since the day he left. He walked away and forgot all about the fact he had a daughter.'

'That's not right.' Julie frowned.

'That *isn't* right,' Jared said emphatically.

'Daddy wouldn't turn his back on any child, let alone his *own* child.'

I'd had enough and stood up. 'Believe what you will. I couldn't care less. I don't have to prove anything to any of you and I don't intend to start trying. I don't belong in this country, this house, or this family. I should never have come here and the sooner I leave, the better it will be for all of us.'

Snatching up my bag, I marched out through the front door with my head held high and unshed tears burning my eyes, filled only with a grim determination to get the hell back to England as soon as ever I could.

Of all people it was Jared who came after me, though I was quite sure it was the last thing he would have wanted to do.

'Won't you come back inside – please?' he added as an afterthought.

'I will not be called a liar or listen to you all defending Saint Mitchell bloody Browning, who was quite obviously beyond reproach in your eyes,' I said furiously.

'You have to forgive us if we find it difficult – if not impossible – to accept the man we knew and loved could ever turn his back on his own flesh and blood.'

'At least you knew him,' I said, uncaring that my tone was harsh and extremely bitter. 'I was never given that opportunity.'

'Will you come back inside? It's cold out here and we should talk about this.'

'We?' I turned on him furiously. 'Why should you care? You've made it crystal clear from the very start that you don't want me here. You've barely been able to bring yourself to be civil to me up to now, so I'll save you the trouble of starting. Go on, go back inside to your family and your happy memories.' I started to walk away.

'At least let me give you a lift somewhere.'

I turned round quickly. 'Back to your aunt's house and then to the airport? I'll wait there until a flight becomes available.'

'If that's what you want.'

'Believe me, it's *exactly* what I want.'

Jared opened the passenger door of his huge car and I climbed inside. Julie had appeared at the front door looking extremely anxious and I could see Ashlyn peering over her shoulder.

'Go back inside and leave this to me,' he said to them, in a tone that brooked no argument, before taking his place on the driver's side of the vehicle and starting the engine.

I was so glad of the warmth that began creeping from the heater almost immediately – though I wouldn't have admitted it for the world. In truth the day had turned cloudy and my jacket was too flimsy to offer any real protection against the chill while I was standing outside of the house.

We'd been driving for a little while when it dawned on me

that we should have reached Julie's house some time ago. I refused to show any concern, though I did wonder what Jared's game was. I'd have put money on him being only too keen to see me on the very next plane out of Victoria.

I risked a little peep at him and was disconcerted to find him looking back at me – and he was smiling. I stared at him, straight-faced.

'I'm not kidnapping you,' he said. 'That's what you're thinking though, right?'

'I wasn't,' I returned truthfully, 'not for a minute. Though I am wondering what you're playing at. You've made it clear you're as keen to see the back of me as I am to go, so why the delay?'

'I thought we should talk.'

With that he turned the wheel and the huge car swept off the road and into a car park high above the sea which sparkled for as far as the eye could see. The views were spectacular, with the blue of the sky reflected in the water and little islands dotted here and there out in the bay.

I hadn't realized this part of Canada offered such beauty, but refused to show that I was impressed and forced myself to look straight at Jared and not back out of the window.

'Talk about what?'

'About what the hell has been going on here, because I don't think everything is as clear cut as you seem to think it is.'

'How much more clear cut could it be?' I demanded bitterly. 'My father left me – and apparently England, too – almost forty years ago and I never saw or heard from him again.'

'Did your mother ever talk to you about what happened?'

'Only to tell me he was gone on the day he left and that he wouldn't be coming back. She was obviously absolutely devastated and refused to mention his name ever again. Who could blame her? I soon learned the whole subject of my father was taboo. Probably, there was nothing she could have told me anyway. He left and that was that.'

'Did your mother ever remarry?'

I nodded.

'What was your stepfather like?'

I shrugged, 'Roy was – and is – a nice enough man, pretty genuine. He's always treated me well, but I was very aware that it was my mother he married and was given no choice but to accept me as part of the package. I couldn't and didn't expect him to love me – after all why would he make the effort when my own father found it impossible? In fairness, I made no attempt to get close to him, either.'

'In case he left you, too, right?' Jared's gaze was steady, and I stared back at him, struck momentarily dumb because I had honestly never really thought of it that way. 'That's how I felt about Mitch for a very long time,' he said quietly.

'But your father died – it's not as if he had a choice about leaving.'

'He still left me.'

I nodded. 'Yes, he did, didn't he? Something like that can really screw up your life.'

'If you let it.'

I suddenly felt as if it was time to be honest and tried not to think too much about exactly whom I was baring my soul to. I did know why. It was because Jared was the first person

– the very first in all these years to show even a glimmer of understanding of how the events in my early life had affected me.

'I think I have let it. I think my mistrust of men has soured every relationship I've ever had and when I eventually married it was for all the wrong reasons. I'm surprised the marriage lasted as long as it did.'

'I'm sorry.' Jared sounded sincere.

'It wasn't just that he left, you see.' I couldn't seem to shut up now that I'd started, 'It was that I never knew *why* or what I had done wrong to make him forget all about me so easily.'

There was a flash of something, anger maybe, on Jared's face. He opened his mouth to say something, and then seemed to think better of it. Reaching out he started the car, saying, 'There's something I think you should see,' and the tyres squealed as he pulled away.

I went to protest when we pulled up before Cheryl's neat house again, but Jared said simply, 'Trust me,' and I found to my amazement that I did.

Cheryl opened the door before we reached it and stood to one side as we walked in. There was no sign of Julie or Ashlyn.

Jared put a hand on his mother's shoulder. 'I think you should show Francesca the box, Mom.'

Without a word she left the room and returned with a big square cardboard box, placing it on the table that had held the tea things earlier. On the top my name, Francesca, was written in bold felt tip pen. I stood and stared, unable to bring myself to touch the box, never mind to open it. Cheryl had no such reservations and reaching inside she picked up a handful of photographs and began to spread them out on the table.

'I always said he should put them into albums or frames, but he never did,' she said, adding sadly, 'just shut himself away and spent time looking at them from time to time.'

To say I was shocked would have been a huge understatement because the pictures were all of me. Some were when I was a baby, a toddler, at school, in my teens – there was even one taken on my wedding day. When curiosity overcame me and I looked into the box I saw there were letters, too, and they were all in my mother's handwriting.

4

The slight crunch as the wheels hit the runway jolted me out of an uncomfortable reverie that had occupied my mind for almost the whole of the long flight back to England. The holiday – if you could call it that – was well and truly over. A part of me still wished I had never made the trip to Canada, but another, more sensible part finally accepted the journey to the truth had been a long time overdue.

I now had more information about my father and his life – and about our relationship, or the lack of one – than I knew what to do with. What was of far more importance, was that I now knew what, or should I say who, had been the cause of the breakdown in communication between my father and me. It was information I wasn't quite sure what to do with yet, but I did know that I had to do something, because the one thing I couldn't do was to ignore it.

'Francesca.'

I blinked, still bleary from the long flight and muzzy-headed with the overload of knowledge I was carrying. I must have imagined that someone had called my name because I certainly wasn't expecting anyone to be meeting me. The sea of smiling faces around the barriers bobbed and weaved in front of my unsteady gaze and I gripped the handle of my trolley more firmly.

'Francesca.'

A firmer and rather larger hand than mine grasped the handle and took over the pushing, while the other arm pulled me close and a light kiss was dropped onto my brow.

Confused I stared up at the man who was my now very *ex*-husband foolishly. 'Adrian, what are you doing here? How did you know…?'

'What plane you'd be coming back on? You asked me to pick up the post and feed the cat while you were gone and I found the number by the phone. Spoke to a very nice woman called Julie.'

I was torn between anger that he had interfered, as usual – in the way I found irritating in the extreme and Adrian saw only as caring – and relieved that I didn't have to find a taxi. In the end it seemed easier to go for the latter, I was far too tired to start looking for an argument never mind a taxi now that I didn't have to, but was also determined to make sure I retrieved my spare door key as soon as it was polite to do so.

'So,' he looked down at me, fair hair flopping boyishly into blue eyes that were bright with barely concealed curiosity, 'Was the trip as illuminating as you'd hoped.'

'Did Julie not tell you anything?' I asked, trying to recall exactly how much I had told him. It couldn't have been much beyond the fact that my father was dead and there was going to be a service in his memory in Canada, since that was all I had been told myself.

'Oh, no, not a thing, not even when I told her I was your husband.' Adrian sounded most indignant.

'*Ex*-husband,' I said with heavy emphasis, pleased that Julie had been so discreet about my family affairs. There would be a detailed discussion when the time was right, but only with the appropriate person. That person wouldn't be Adrian – despite the life we had once shared. 'There's nothing much to tell beyond what you already know. I hope you haven't spoken to anyone else about this.'

'Your mother, you mean? No, I wouldn't do that when you expressly asked me not to. Joan will have to be told, you know.'

'Yes,' I agreed, a little sharply, 'and I will speak to her in my own good time.'

I watched him feeding coins into the parking machine and wondered – possibly as a result of my conversation with Jared – if all that had gone wrong between us was entirely my fault. Marrying for the wrong reasons was always going to be a bad idea but I had thought that marriage and a family of my own would heal the hurt of the past.

To start with I had loved the constant phone calls and the way Adrian always wanted to know where I was and what I was doing at any given time. It had seemed so romantic that he always met me from work with flowers and plans for the evening, and didn't all couples spend their weekends together? It was a fact that I had probably mistaken Adrian's increasing jealousy and possessiveness for love and had spent far too long trying to mould myself into what he wanted me to be, dreading that otherwise he might leave me, too. I still found it hard to believe that in the end I was the one who had walked away.

Adrian never could quite understand why our marriage hadn't worked and would never accept that his own behaviour had played a huge part in my decision to leave. Having a family might have made a difference, but the time was never right for Adrian and as the years slipped by I became as lonely in my marriage as I had been in my childhood. He always said having me was enough for him – unfortunately, he wasn't enough for me and in the end I had to be honest enough to say so.

I confess to being surprised that Adrian didn't do more to make me stay, but had my suspicions that he thought I would soon see the error of my ways. I think we were both a little shocked when eventually the divorce went through on the grounds of our separation. I didn't regret the end of my marriage, but I did regret hurting someone who – after all – was only being himself. As a result I spent a lot of time wondering if there was something of my fickle father in me, after all.

My luggage was stowed into the boot of Adrian's navy blue BMW and I was helped into the front passenger seat as if I was a hundred and three years old instead of a mere forty-three. I swallowed my irritation and smiled at Adrian as he climbed behind the wheel.

'This is very kind of you,' I said, 'taking time off work.'

'You know I'll always be here for you,' he said kindly and patted my hand.

As if to prove his point he insisted on carrying my luggage, not only to my door but right inside, where he then bustled round putting the kettle on and feeding the cat. Both were things I had been looking forward to doing myself – and by myself. I knew it would be difficult to budge him and I was proved right, but what could I say when he had gone to so much trouble? There were even fresh flowers and groceries.

I felt I had no choice but to accept Adrian's offer to prepare a meal. After all, when he'd bought the food I could hardly refuse his offer to cook it. I felt mean-spirited and ungrateful for wishing him elsewhere but found myself shuddering when I realized he had, once again, turned an offer of help into an invitation to ingrate himself back into my life and start taking control.

I couldn't have dropped more hints about jet lag if I had tried, had been yawning for England for the past two hours, and still he stayed fussing around, washing up, wiping down counter tops, until I could have screamed. I began to feel that if I didn't show him the door soon he would have my suitcase emptied and a full load of washing on. There was nothing for it but to be blunt.

I stretched and yawned again, a huge exaggerated and drawn out affair that should have given the hint to the most thick-skinned individual. I hadn't expected it to work, so wasn't at all surprised when it didn't.

'Sorry, Adrian, but I'm going to have to ask you to leave. I'm really grateful for all of your help, you've been marvellous, but I do need my bed.'

'Oh, you go right ahead,' he encouraged, 'I'll just tidy up a bit more, you won't even know that I'm here.'

'No,' my tone was more abrupt than I would have liked, but I'd really had enough of his cosseting. 'You go. Really. I can manage now.'

He looked hurt, just as I'd known he would, but there was

a familiar edge of annoyance in his tone. 'I just thought, you know, your first day back….'

'I'll be fine on my own now, but thank you for your kind thought in meeting me and for the meal – it was very nice.'

He rolled down his sleeves and put his suit jacket on, his stiff movements and rigid back showed that he was prepared to be deeply offended. I did my best to ignore the familiar guilt I could feel creeping in and pointedly moved towards the door to let him out, putting my hand out at the last minute and reminding him, 'The key, please, Adrian.'

I looked at the cat as the door banged behind him, and she looked back at me. There was a pained expression on her sweet face, though she might just have been hungry again.

'Oh, dear, Ellie,' I pulled a rueful face, 'I think we'll have to find someone else to feed you when I'm away in future.' For a long moment she stared at me with accusing amber eyes and then with a swish of her tortoise-shell tail she disappeared through the cat flap. So, I sighed deeply, that was two of them I'd managed to mortally offend and I hadn't been home much more than five minutes. Deciding I might just as well go for the jackpot I reached for the phone.

Unusually, it was my stepfather who answered the phone demanding, the moment he heard my voice, 'Where on earth have you been? Your mother's been frantic.'

'Why?' It seemed a perfectly reasonable response to me, since we were hardly in what you would call frequent contact, especially when they were ensconced in their holiday home in Spain. They had their life and I had mine, we spoke probably once a month if that.

'What do you mean – why? Joan's been calling and calling you?'

'Why?' I asked again.

He seemed at a loss for a moment and then blustered a bit, before admitting, 'I'm not actually sure. She got a letter and said she had to speak to you right away. Why don't you have a bloody answerphone like everybody else?'

'I do, actually,' I said calmly, 'I just don't choose to use it.' I didn't feel obliged to go on and explain that I'd become sick and tired of deleting numerous messages from my ex-husband all saying the same thing, 'Just checking that you're all right, Francesca.'

'Can I speak to her, then?' I tried to hurry the process along.

'Who?'

Honestly, sometimes it was like wading through treacle trying to get through to my stepfather. I wondered if he was getting worse or whether it was just that I ran out of patience sooner these days. I resisted the urge to scream but only with difficulty.

'Mum, of course. Who else would I mean? Is she there?'

'I thought I just told you. She's on her way back to England again – in a car to the airport as we speak. She hasn't that long been back in Spain. At this rate I'd just as well pack up and come back, too. We'd have been there already but the weather over there in England hasn't been up to much, has it? Do you know what it's about?'

The question took me by surprise because I was only just processing the information that my mother was, apparently, on her way here. It must be the jet lag, I decided. Why my stepfather should think I would know anything about my mother's reasons for travelling back and forth I had absolutely no idea. They were the ones living in each other's pockets, just as they always had done. I couldn't for the life of me imagine why my mother would want to discuss something with me before her own husband.

It was about that moment that the penny dropped with a deafening clang. She'd received a letter, the contents of which she chose not to share with the man she lived with, but was prepared to jump into a plane and fly round the globe to discuss with me. The letter obviously must have contained the news of my father's death, though why the haste to share this information when she had withheld everything else about his life from me was quite beyond me. The conversation was going to be interesting to say the least – especially as she would have no idea just how much I already knew. I had a strong feeling the Browning family would have given her only the bare facts – that was all she'd given my father all these years, after all.

'I have no idea,' I told my stepfather briskly, 'but you'd better tell me what flight Mum will be on so that I can meet her when she arrives.'

'Oh, she's already phoned Adrian. He'll be meeting the flight.'

I raised my eyes to heaven and gritted my teeth until they hurt. When would she realize Adrian was no longer her son-in-law and not at her beck and call. I was about to say as much to my stepfather, and then I realized it was a definite case of the pot calling the kettle black. I should also stop looking upon my ex-husband as an easy option and start managing on my own. Between us, it was no wonder Adrian still saw himself as a member of this family.

'Well, at least tell me when the flight is due in, so I have a rough idea of what time to expect Mum to arrive here. If she decides to stay with me I'll need to make up the spare bed.'

After I put the phone down, I wondered if Adrian had already known about the second trip to the airport when he collected me and decided immediately that he would have done. His reason for not sharing the news was that he knew full well that I'd have insisted on meeting the flight myself. This way he had the perfect excuse to return and show me how indispensable he was to my family and to me. How galling when I had practically thrown him out earlier and I don't know why I was even surprised to find that he'd already made up the bed in the spare room.

It felt as if I'd only just fallen asleep when the rattle of the letterbox woke me. Before I could move my mother's voice pierced the gloom of early evening, 'Franny, Franny, are you there?'

'I'm coming, I'm coming,' I called, struggling to get up in a hurry before she managed to wrench the flap from the door.

'Franny,' my mother threw herself into my arms in a most uncharacteristic way.

I automatically drew her close patting her shoulder awkwardly and doing my best to ignore the smug and rather self-important look on Adrian's face.

'I'll just bring the bags in, shall I?' he asked knowing full well I could do nothing but agree with a grudging, 'Thank you.'

He looked as if he was quite prepared to out-stay his welcome all over again, but it seemed – for once – my mother was as keen to see the back of him as I was. She was rather more subtle about it than I had been previously, just saying how tired she was after the flight and how we had, 'things to discuss if he didn't mind,' so that Adrian had little choice but to make himself scarce. His disappointment and annoyance was palpable.

'Such a lovely man,' my mother said regretfully, 'such a shame – is there no chance...?'

'None, Mum,' I said flatly, 'so let's not even waste time discussing it.'

I made tea and came back to find Mum looking around with interest, realizing it was the first time she'd seen the flat I'd bought with my share of the proceeds from the marital home.

'It's nice,' she nodded approvingly, 'and the garden goes with it, does it?' She peered through the patio door to the darkened garden beyond.

'Yes. Just big enough and lovely when the sun shines.'

My mother shuddered. 'Which is not often enough to my mind. Buying a holiday home and moving to Spain in the cold months was the best decision Roy and I ever made.'

'So what brings you back now, then? It's only May and has barely warmed up yet.'

I was careful not to look at my mother but gave all my attention to pouring the tea.

Finally, finally, the truth was going to come out. Finally I was going to learn why my mother had made the decision to shut my father out of my life, to deny him access or any contact through the mail or phone. She had apparently made it clear I was not allowed to receive presents or cards from him and yet, cruelly, she'd kept him up to date with my progress through life with regular photos and progress reports. The only contact he had had been through her.

I could feel it – the anger building up inside of me like a volcano about to erupt. I had been suppressing it since the box of my life had been put in front of me in Canada and I had realized that the lack of any communication between my father and me had not been of his making – and it certainly had not been through his choice.

I stared at the top of my mother's bowed head, saw the silver strands in the dark hair that she still wore far too long for a woman of her age, and willed her to just come out and say it. Somehow, she had to tell me how it was and try to justify her actions. She was my mother and I loved her in my own way, but I didn't think I would ever forgive her for depriving me of my father's love.

'I've had a letter,' she began, and there was a sob in her voice. I wondered whom exactly she was upset for – my father, me or for herself because the truth had finally caught up with her – and felt futile rage begin to engulf me.

'From the hospital,' she continued, and finally lifted a face that was drowning in her tears to look into my eyes. 'I have cancer.'

5

Whatever I had been expecting my mother to say, the words, 'I have cancer,' weren't even close. I floundered for a moment, trying to find a firm footing in a world that had suddenly turned to shifting sand beneath my feet.

'I – What?' I struggled to find something, anything, to say.

'I came over recently for a routine mammogram,' she said, suddenly calm, 'and now I've had this letter calling me back for further tests. The appointment is tomorrow afternoon.'

'Oh, Mum,' I said, trying to sound matter-of-fact when inside I was filled with fear and panic because while we might not be close, she was the only mother I had, 'that happens all the time. It will be nothing, I'm sure.'

'Has it happened to you?' she asked quickly.

'Well, no, because they don't do routine mammograms until you're pushing fifty and I have a way to go yet – remember?'

'They wouldn't call me back for nothing.' She stared at me, but her eyes were already looking beyond me to what the future might hold for her. Her terror was almost tangible.

'It will be all right, Mum. You'll see.' I hoped I sounded

convincing but her fear was contagious. I had just lost one parent and now if the worst came to the worst it appeared that I might be about to lose the other. I couldn't believe life could be so bloody unfair.

'Should I ask Adrian to go with me?' she wondered out loud. 'He's very good in that kind of situation.'

'You should *not*,' I said indignantly. '*I'm* your daughter, *I* will take you.'

'What about work, though? Adrian said something about you being away on holiday when he realized I'd been trying to get hold of you. You didn't tell *me* you were going away.'

'I'm working as a temp at the moment, I'm sure I told you that, so I can work or not as I choose. Do you always tell me what you and Roy are up to? I can barely keep up with your trips backwards and forwards to Spain,' I countered, hoping Adrian hadn't told her anything more, and wishing once again that he wouldn't take such a continuing interest in my life and my family. 'I didn't know that you'd already been over to England until Roy told me.'

She pounced on that. 'You spoke to Roy? When was that?'

I had mentioned that without thinking and I cringed – cursing my big mouth. I waited for her to ask why I was ringing her in Spain, but was relieved when she didn't. Now was definitely not the time to tell her where I'd been on my travels or to start throwing accusations at her about keeping my father from me.

Funny – but not in a humorous way – how the anger about her deceit, that had been so all consuming, had all but disappeared now that I had something else to worry about. I kept telling myself she must have had her reasons – valid reasons to her – for doing what she had and that I would just have to wait to find out what those reasons were.

In the end I decided to offer a vague explanation for the call to Spain in the hope it would make it appear less important, and said, 'It was earlier. Funny that, eh? Me phoning to see how you were when you were already on your way home. Anyway,' I became brisk, 'I think we both need a good night's sleep, so we'd best get ourselves off to bed.'

'Oh, I doubt I'll sleep a wink, Franny. I don't think I've ever been so scared if I'm being honest.'

Taking her hands into mine I was shocked to feel them trembling. I wasn't used to seeing my mother like this but then she was used to being taken care of by the dependable Roy and even Roy couldn't take care of this.

I found it quite upsetting, but still said, 'Please don't feel you have to put on a brave face for me, Mum, but honestly there is no point in worrying ahead. I have some Nytol in the cupboard. It's a natural remedy from the health shop – will you try some of that?'

She looked doubtful as well she might, since I didn't think I'd seen her take as much as an aspirin before in my life, 'Are you taking some?'

'I don't think I'll need it,' I almost mentioned jet lag, then thought of the questions that admission would bring and thought better of it, 'but it won't hurt, so yes, I will take some, too.'

I showed her where everything was; the cosy bedroom she could use and the pretty tiled bathroom opposite with walk-in shower. Helping to unpack her suitcase, I couldn't help noticing the unusually haphazard way the clothes had been thrust in, leaving them crumpled and, in most cases, requiring a damn good press in order to make them wearable. I hung the garments up without comment, telling myself some of the creases might have dropped out by morning.

'It is a very nice place,' she allowed again but still with a trace of reluctance in her tone, 'better than the place you rented for a while.'

'I think so,' I said, pleased with the compliment and realizing how hard it must have been for her to pay it. 'I know it's not the three-bedroom house I lived in with Adrian, but it's mine and I'm happy here. It's sad that our relationship didn't work out in the end but not all marriages last forever as I'm sure you understand,' I added.

'Yes, but ...'

'There are no buts, Mum. It's over, we're divorced now and it's no longer up for discussion.'

There was a welcome distraction as Ellie suddenly leaped through the window I'd opened to let some air in and we both jumped.

'Oh, my God,' my mother clasped a hand to her throat, 'that made me jump. Is it your cat?'

'Yes, pretty, isn't she? Adrian's been coming in to see to her. I got her from the Cat's Protection.' I called her over, tickled the furry chin and was rewarded with a huge rumbling purr. 'I could never have a cat before because of Adrian's allergies.'

'But I thought you just said he was feeding her for you while you were away,' my mother sounded vaguely confused.

'Mmm,' I tried to sound non-committal. In fairness,

popping in to feed an animal once a day wasn't the same as living with one, but I had always had my suspicions that Adrian's allergies had been another way of taking control. He hadn't wanted us to have a pet and had found a way to make sure we never did. 'I would close your door tonight if you don't want to find her sharing your bed.'

'I would never have imagined you with an animal,' she shook her head.

I only just refrained from reminding her of all the Christmases I had pleaded with Santa Claus to send me a pet of my own to love. I wondered now if subconsciously I had been looking, even then, or perhaps especially then, for something to fill the gaping hole my father leaving had left behind. The day I realized he had gone was the day I first understood – even at four years old – what loneliness really meant. It was a feeling that had never truly left me if I was honest with myself. Nothing and no one had ever really taken his place – and probably never would now that he was gone.

I was awake early the following morning but my mother must have woken even earlier because I found her sitting at the kitchen table gazing into a cup of tea I was pretty sure was stone cold.

'I didn't wake you, did I?' she said, at the same time as I asked, 'Have you been here all night?'

'No,' I said and 'No,' she said, and we managed a little laugh apiece that lacked any hint of humour.

She was wrapped in the shabby blue towelling robe I kept behind the bathroom door and an attempt had obviously been made the night before to wrap her dark hair around ancient sponge curlers, but long strands were escaping and trailed to her hunched shoulders. Devoid of make-up she looked pale and the dark shadows under her eyes showed the strain she was under. For the first time I thought she looked far older than her sixty-one years and that frightened me and made me feel protective of her in a way I never had before.

'I'll make some fresh tea, shall I?' I bustled about, focusing on practicalities. 'Have you eaten anything?'

'Tea would be nice.' She looked at the cup she was holding, as if seeing it for the first time. 'I think this has gone cold. I don't think I can eat anything, though. I actually feel a bit sick.'

'Just try a piece of toast, or I could boil you an egg to go with it?'

My mother shook her head, still staring at the cup, and then she looked up suddenly and straight at me. 'What do you think they've found?' she asked. 'The letter didn't say too much.'

I could only reply, 'I don't know, Mum, I really don't know.'

I made toast that we made a poor pretence of eating. The newspaper I picked up from the doormat seemed to hold far too many references to breast and every other kind of cancer, from frightening statistics to yet another celebrity death from the disease. After a quick look I folded the pages carefully so that a report on global warming was uppermost and tried to make a joke about being disappointed that the heat we'd been promised as a result of the greenhouse effect had never materialized.

'The weather is the least of my worries at the moment,' she said flatly, and the conversation ground to a halt again.

We got ready, though it was far too early, which gave me the chance to press the dress she was wearing and I found myself offering, 'Would you like me to do your hair?' purely as another means of passing the time.

She looked much better when I had finished pinning it up, and couldn't have been aware of how close to tears the hint of roots that were as white as snow had made me. I had to keep reminding myself that early sixties wasn't old and neither did a suspect mammogram mean my mother definitely had cancer.

It was as if she read my mind. 'I'm being silly, aren't I?' She was actually smiling at her reflection in the mirror as she said this. 'I think I'll put a bit of make-up on, you know. Make myself feel better. It will turn out to be something and nothing. I'm glad now that I didn't worry Roy.'

By the time we left the hospital, after my mother had endured some sort of needle test and ultrasound, with the appointment for a lumpectomy being arranged, all pretence at bravado was well and truly gone. I knew we had both been hoping to be told, there and then, that there was no problem after all, and the call-back had all been a precautionary measure, an over-reaction instead of another step closer to being told something we really didn't want to hear.

I could only guess at my mother's state of mind, but the smile on her face had become a grimace and the grip on my hand was vice-like as we made our way back to the car. I felt cold to my bones and very, very afraid, both for her and for myself. Losing the father I hadn't known had been one thing, I decided, but the thought of losing the mother I loved despite our, sometimes difficult, relationship was quite something else. Whatever she had or hadn't done, I forgave her there and then. I didn't know what else I could do under those sort of circumstances.

Human nature has amazing powers of recovery though, and by the time we got back to my place we were assuring each other further tests still didn't mean anything, and were simply a precautionary measure. This was what I told Roy – against my mother's wishes – when he phoned.

'You can't keep him in the dark,' I'd insisted, 'it's just not fair and it's not right. He will be very angry and very hurt when he finds out, as he surely will, sooner or later.'

The poor man was horrified. 'Why didn't she tell me? I'm her husband, I should have been told.'

'Yes, you should have been,' I agreed, 'but I don't think Mum was thinking straight and some things are easier to share with another woman.'

'I suppose so,' he agreed grudgingly. 'I'm coming straight home. I want to be there for her, make sure she gets the very best of care – whatever it costs.'

This, coming from a man who all through my childhood had re-used tea bags and gone around switching off lights so diligently that you would often find yourself sitting in the dark, made me realize Roy was taking this very seriously. I guessed penny-pinching suddenly didn't seem so important to him any more.

'Can I talk to her?'

I looked across to where my mother was sitting, still

huddled in her coat and correctly interpreting the request, she shook her head. 'She's resting right now.' The lie came easily to my lips because my only concern at that moment was for my mother and her wishes.

'I'll pack up as soon as I can. When is Joan's next appointment?'

I assured him we would let him know the minute we heard anything, and that the NHS care my mother was receiving couldn't be faulted, but he was still huffing and puffing his concern when I put the receiver down.

'Can I stay here until Roy arrives? I don't want to be left alone with time to think.'

I went and sat close beside her and took her freezing hand into mine. 'You can stay as long as you want,' I said. 'I like having you here and I just wish it hadn't taken something like this to bring us closer together.'

She clung to me in a way that was foreign to her. My mother had never been a demonstrative woman and, consequently, neither had I. I'm sure that both Roy and Adrian would have preferred it to have been otherwise.

I hugged her close and she didn't resist. 'In fact, now that we can spend some time together, why don't we make the most of it? Enjoy some of that quality time we've been missing out on.'

The sudden smile lit up her face, 'I'd like that.'

'We'll spoil ourselves for the rest of today.' I found myself full of enthusiasm, and rushed on, 'Put our feet up and watch a DVD....'

'In the middle of the day?' My mother sounded scandalized.

I laughed. 'Is there a law against watching a film in daylight hours?'

'Well, I suppose not, if you put it like that. Can we have a takeaway, too? Roy hates fast food but I love it and I do get sick of cooking.'

I laughed, 'It's your choice then. And tomorrow we'll go shopping and perhaps get our nails done.'

I watched her clap her hands like an excited little girl and was glad I'd thought of it. It was a long time since I'd treated myself, and a whole lot longer since I'd treated my mother to anything more than dutiful birthday and Christmas presents at the appropriate times.

For the time being I had to put all thoughts of the past and its secrets away, and just concentrate on the present. I didn't need to remind myself again that my father was already dead or that my mother might soon be facing her own struggle for life. This was no time for recriminations.

We ate huge slices of pizza with melted cheese trailing from our chins, and alternately laughed and cried our way through *Marley and Me*, the story of a wayward dog. I had thought that a safe choice of entertainment, forgetting about the miscarried baby bit, but at least there was no hint of the 'C' word. I was well aware that my mother's favourite film was and always had been, *Love Story*, and carefully hid my copy behind a pile of books before I let her choose a second film to watch.

Of all things, she chose *The Full Monty*, grinning at me as she said, 'I always wanted to see what all the fuss was about, but Roy wouldn't hear of it. Aren't men funny?'

'Adrian wouldn't have it in the house, either, but it's actually a great story and not even particularly rude.'

It was as if mentioning his name had conjured him up because the next minute the phone rang and he said in a deeply concerned tone, 'Just phoning to see how you both are.'

'We're fine,' I said firmly, 'and you've just caught us setting off to see a film.'

'Oh,' he sounded taken aback, 'Can I give you a lift?'

'No, we don't need a lift but thank you for offering – and for ringing. Now, shouldn't you be managing a project, or something?'

My mother looked shocked as I replaced the receiver and then she giggled girlishly, 'Ooh, you are naughty.'

I held up the DVD. 'I didn't lie, did I? Here's the film and we don't need a lift. If I'd said we were staying in he'd have turned up on some pretext and sat between us tutting all the way through *The Full Monty*.'

'He has a good heart,' my mother defended him. 'I thought you loved him.'

'So did I for a very long time, but we all make mistakes, don't we?'

I held my breath, wondering if she would admit that marrying my father had been a mistake, for him if not for her.

'I suppose so,' was all she said and the moment passed.

Laughter must be every bit as good for us as the experts say because we went to bed in a much happier frame of mind, waking in exactly the right mood to face a day of pampering and retail therapy.

'Let's pretend we're on one of those make-over shows,' I suggested, 'and we'll start with "before" photos taken on my digital camera and end the day with "after" ones to see how they compare.'

We decided that 'before' photos always showed the subject looking miserable, without hair or make-up done and that we should go along with that to make the change all the more startling.

'I'm not taking my teeth out, though,' my mother insisted, 'not for anybody.'

'You don't have false teeth,' I was shocked, 'do you?'

'One or two,' she admitted, 'but even Roy hasn't seen me without them. If I have to have an operation they will have to go back in as soon as I open my eyes and before I get any visitors.'

The thought of an operation wiped any hint of a smile from our faces to give perfect 'before' pictures, but viewing them sent us into fits of laughter and the moment was forgotten again as we hurried to make ourselves presentable before we left the house.

Because we'd left home so early we had plenty of time and to my amazement after a manicure and pedicure my mother agreed to a hair appointment when the same beauty parlour said they could fit us both in. I warned myself not to expect too much since this was a woman who had never had her hair expertly cut to my certain knowledge, but dealt with any irregular trims herself or left them in the inexpert hands of friends and neighbours.

'Just cut straight across the bottom,' she'd say carelessly, and then would slice a crooked path across the fringe to finish off.

I'd always refused absolutely to take up the scissors on her behalf and had long given up making appointments with reputable hairdressers that she would never keep, so to say I was gobsmacked when she finally appeared was a massive understatement.

I could feel my mouth drop open. 'Mum,' I said, 'is that you?'

She flicked her shoulder-length bob, and laughed, 'I don't look that different, do I?'

'You look,' I replied and could hear the reverence in my tone, 'absolutely beautiful. That cut has taken years off you and the lighter colour really suits your skin tone.'

'That's what the stylist said,' my mother nodded, checking her reflection in the mirror and flicking her hair a bit more.

Even the eye-watering bill for the two of us seemed a small price to pay for the radical transformation in at least one of us. I was more than happy to pay up, smiling over my lightened purse when my mother practically skipped out into the street.

After lunch she jumped at my suggestion of a new outfit to compliment the look and practically dragged me into M & S. I had never seen her so excited over clothes before. As frugal as Roy, my mother had never spent two pence on herself if one would do and yet she was an attractive woman when she made the effort – as I was hoping today would prove to her.

I was exhausted at the end of the day, just from trying to keep up with her, but thrilled, too, on her behalf and more than happy to share the expense or even to meet it all.

'Nonsense,' she handed over her debit card with a flourish.

'I've suddenly realized the pointlessness of money sitting in the bank. It's time I started living.'

She didn't say, 'While I still can,' but the words hung in the air between us, and I felt an ice-cold shiver run the full length of my spine.

Roy was waiting, not very patiently, on my doorstep when we got back. To his credit, he didn't even blink at the huge array of carrier bags, but scooped them and my mother into his car. If he'd noticed her new look he wasn't saying so and it was left to me to run and fetch her suitcase from my spare bedroom.

'Let's get you home,' he said, 'where I can take care of you. I went there first and I've put the heating and lights on and drawn all the curtains. Thank you, Francesca, I appreciate what you've done for your mother, but I can take over now.'

I wanted to argue but knew I didn't have a leg to stand on. We had lived our separate lives for too long now, but I still made a phone sign with my fingers and mouthed, 'Ring me,' to my mother, and then they were gone. It was only then I realized we'd never had the chance to take our 'after' photos.

I hadn't been inside five minutes, in fact I had fed the cat but not yet removed my coat, when the doorbell rang – and rang – as if someone were leaning on the bell press.

I hurried to answer it. The urgency of the strident sound hinted at an emergency and I could only think my mother had collapsed in the car and Roy had immediately turned back. If that wasn't the case and it was Adrian on one of his far too frequent visits, I had already decided that he was going to get the sharp edge of my tongue.

The bell was still ringing when I threw back the door with my imagination working overtime. What I hadn't imagined – not in a million years – was finding Jared what-ever-his name-was on my doorstep.

6

I barely had a moment to take in the tall, dark and all too familiar figure filling my doorway and wearing the scowl that was equally familiar, before Jared was demanding, 'Where is she?' in that high-handed way of his.

'Roy came and collected her,' I said, wondering what on earth he wanted with my mother and why he looked so angry. Surely he hadn't come all this way to have a go at her on my behalf for the truth she had kept concealed about my father.

'Roy?' he practically roared the name. 'Who the hell is Roy?'

'Don't you *dare* shout at me like that,' I said furiously, reminding myself that he was in *my* country now and on the step of *my* home. 'Roy is my stepfather, my mother's husband. Who else would she be with?'

A look of total confusion settled on Jared's face. 'She came here and you've sent her away with this Roy – but why?'

'I didn't send her away,' I explained patiently, even while I was questioning why I was bothering. What the hell it had to do with Jared where my mother was and who she was with,

I really had no idea. 'She was here until my stepfather arrived back from Spain and could take her home.'

'But she's *your* sister. Ashlyn has nothing to do with your family, so why would you send her to stay with them.'

'Ashlyn?' I stared up at him, now totally confused myself. 'She hasn't been here. I thought we were talking about my mother, who has just left.'

Jared's shoulders seemed to slump and all the anger in him appeared to drain away, leaving him grey-faced and clearly deeply concerned – obviously about Ashlyn, though I had no idea why.

'You'd better come in.' I stood back and opened the door wider.

He filled my small sitting room in a way my mother never had, or Adrian either come to that. Without asking he removed his leather jacket and draped it over the back of an armchair.

'Can I get you a coffee?' I felt obliged to offer, 'Or perhaps something stronger?'

Collapsing into the chair, he leaned forward, and buried his head into his hands. Ignoring my question, he said, 'I was so sure, so bloody certain, she would be here.'

'Why?'

'Ashlyn has talked of nothing and no one else since you left Canada. She's missing and so is her passport. I know she had discussed applying for a place at university here in the UK with her – your – father before he died. I'm sure they already had it planned that she would come looking for you. I just assumed....'

He looked up then, and in spite of myself my heart went out to him. He was obviously very afraid for his sister, and I didn't blame him. I barely knew the girl and I was concerned. She was eighteen years old, if that, and probably alone in what was a dangerous world. Ashlyn could be anywhere and worse – she could be with anybody.

Trying to be sensible and not jump to conclusions, I said, 'You assumed she would be here, but do you know for a fact she's even left Canada?'

'The minute we realized she had gone, we contacted everyone – and I do mean everyone – who knows her. All of her friends are of the opinion she would be heading for England. If she isn't in the UK, then I don't even know where else to start looking.'

'Ashlyn isn't here. I would tell you if she was, even if I didn't feel obliged to tell you where. This is too serious to be playing games. Do you think she might have already made an application through the UCAS system to universities in this country?'

Jared shrugged, 'That's something she might have shared with Mitch, but not with me or with our mother.'

'Any idea what course she might be interested in applying for?'

He brightened imperceptibly, 'Social work is all she's ever wanted to do and because of the family's long history of fostering she's had contact with social workers from an early age. She's studied all the right subjects at school and gained so much relevant experience with homeless people and kids with disabilities. I know I'm biased but …'

Jared sounded so proud of his sister and I couldn't help but be impressed myself, not many eighteen-year-olds showed such determination.

'The thing is, of all the universities she may or may not have applied to, it's a hell of a long shot that Ashlyn would even have applied locally for a place. Brankstone is one of the newer universities after all. You also have to remember, Jared, that Ashlyn is technically an adult and is quite entitled to go wherever she likes at home or abroad.'

The familiar frown was back in place. 'She's just a kid.'

'To you, she is just a kid. I'm not sure if Ashlyn would agree.'

'Yes, but—'

'We can argue until we're blue in the face. It won't change a thing. If you're right, and Ashlyn is in the UK and looking for me – she will turn up sooner or later – I promise I will let you know if she does.' I paused torn between good manners and a strong wish to be rid of my uninvited and unwanted visitor. It had been a long day and I was both tired and hungry.

I cursed the polite behaviour that had been instilled into me from the time I was a small child because when I opened my mouth to say I would show Jared out, instead I heard myself say, 'Well, I don't know about you, but I'm starving. I'm not the best cook in the world, but I can rustle up an omelette apiece if you're interested.'

He hesitated, and I felt a rush of relief as I quickly suggested, 'You have other plans, of course.'

'I should ...'

Jared got to his feet and I got ready to hand him his jacket, trying not to look as if I was eager to get rid of him. I wasn't sure why I was being so careful of his feelings, since he hadn't always been so careful of mine.

'No, you're right.' He sat down again and I realized that my relief at the thought of seeing the back of him had been premature.

'I am?' I said.

'She'll either turn up, or she won't and me rushing around like a lunatic trying to guess where she might be won't help either way.'

'I'll go and whip up some eggs,' I said with a distinct lack of enthusiasm.

'Can I help?'

The last thing I wanted was to be tripping over him in my tiny kitchen. 'No,' I said shortly, 'I can manage.' Through gritted teeth I added, 'Why don't you make yourself at home.'

Jared obviously took me at my word, because when I eventually came back with the food steaming on the plates I carried in each hand, he was sound asleep with the disloyal Ellie curled up on his lap.

He looked so peaceful, almost human in fact, with the frown lines smoothed away, that I left him there and tiptoed back to the kitchen to place his omelette in the oven to keep warm and settled down to eat my own in peace.

He didn't sleep for long and when I peeped round the door to check he was already stirring, looking around him in a moment of evident confusion, especially when he saw the cat.

'Where am I?' he said to himself and then to the cat, 'and where did you come from?'

'She's mine,' I said, stepping right into the room, 'her name's Ellie. Now, are you ready for that omelette? If it stays in the oven much longer it will be like rubber and not fit to eat.'

'Have I been asleep long?'

'Just a few minutes – you looked like you needed it.' I shooed the cat down and placed a tray on Jared's lap, then sort of hovered offering bread and butter, coffee or tea, while he ate with far more enthusiasm than my simple offering deserved.

'Thank you,' he said, sitting back with a sigh, 'for the meal and for the common sense. I know in my heart you're right about Ashlyn. It's her life and she will do what she wants, but I can't help feeling responsible for her since Mitch died.'

'She's lucky to have someone to look out for her,' I said, and meant it. Ashlyn had not only grown up with my father, but with the sibling I had always wanted, too. I tried not to envy her, but it wasn't easy.

Jared seemed in no hurry to leave, but it was getting to the point that I wanted my home to myself again. So much had happened in a very short time, and I hadn't even begun to come to terms with most of it. I had always needed time alone – something my ex-husband had never been able to understand – and never more so than at that moment.

It took all of my willpower not to push him out of the door when he finally made a move, but not before giving me the address of his hotel, the room number and his mobile phone number. When he was gone I leaned back against the door and gave a huge heartfelt sigh of relief.

My relief that day seemed always destined to be short-lived, because almost immediately there was a sharp rap that almost had me jumping out of my skin. Skin, I might add, that was getting thinner by the minute. I couldn't begin to think what he might want now.

Then I had the sudden thought that it might have been Ashlyn waiting close by until her brother had left, and I fumbled hurriedly with the door-catch. She wasn't my concern, I reminded myself, as the door opened, but I couldn't see an eighteen-year-old girl out on the streets in a strange country late at night.

'Adrian?' he would have barged inside if I hadn't stood firmly in his way, 'what on earth do you want?'

'You assured me,' he was saying indignantly, '*assured* me there was no one else in your life.'

'What?' I stared at him, 'When?'

'When you ended our marriage – against my wishes, I might add – you told me there was no one else in your life.'

I couldn't believe we were having this conversation or why and I said so.

'There quite obviously is,' he said indignantly, 'I just saw him leaving with my own eyes and heard him ask you to call him.'

I almost laughed out loud when I realized Adrian was talking about Jared and was about to launch into an explanation when I realized I didn't actually owe him one, and set about telling him so in no uncertain terms.

'How dare you.'

'What?' Obviously taken aback, he stared at me.

'We,' I pointed out, 'are divorced now, as in no longer married, and what I do and who I see are absolutely nothing to do with you any more. Is that clear?'

'But—'

'There is no but. Do I hang around where you live and work? Do I ring to check up on you? Do I turn up on your doorstep on a regular basis? *Do I?*' I demanded more firmly when no answer was forthcoming.

Adrian shook his head and his fair hair, damp now from the rain that had started to fall, drooped disconsolately into his eyes. 'No,' he said.

I relented, but only slightly, and sighed out loud. 'I don't want to be bad friends with you, Adrian, but you have to accept that life moves on.'

'Well, yours obviously has,' he declared bitterly.

'Yes,' I replied firmly and not altogether truthfully – especially in the way he meant, 'it has, and I hope that you can wish me well – as I do you.'

He turned away, but when I went to close the door he turned back and asked pathetically, 'Am I not to contact you – now you have a new boyfriend?'

To refuse him would have been like kicking a puppy. 'It will be nice to hear how you're doing,' I said, adding, 'sometimes.'

The door had barely latched when there was another rap on the wood, and I had just about had enough. So angry that it was a wonder there was no steam coming out of my ears, I flung the door back and had a large piece of my mind all ready prepared to give out.

On the doorstep was a soaking wet Ashlyn holding an equally damp Ellie.

'Can I come in?' she said.

7

'Ashlyn.' I almost dragged her inside and then peered up and down the wet and darkening street as if I expected to see that she'd been followed. By whom, I wasn't quite sure. 'Now, what on earth are you doing here? Everyone at home is worried sick about you.'

To my utter consternation she burst into tears and, dropping the cat, threw herself into my unwilling arms. I held her, kind of awkwardly and limply, but she wasn't having any of that and pulled me to her in a hug so tight I could hardly breathe.

It gave me the strangest feeling – to be held by this girl, this stranger – and it wasn't altogether unpleasant, though I still wouldn't allow myself to even begin to think of her as family or give in and hug her back. I doubt she would have noticed, anyway, since she was clearly totally wrapped up in her own drama.

'I couldn't tell anyone,' her voice came out muffled, her face buried into the wool of my sweater. 'They would only have stopped me coming.'

About to go into the whys and the wherefores, I realized

we were still standing in the hallway, and the flimsy jacket Ashlyn was wearing was, like her long blonde hair, soaking wet.

It almost felt like here-we-go-again, as I said, 'You'd better come on through.'

'You see ...' she began, barely taking in her surroundings in her hurry to give me the facts as she saw them.

'Later,' I put up a hand, 'first a shower and some hot food. You're shivering,' I realized, and hurrying her to the bathroom, I showed her where everything was and left her to it. It really was the least I could do for the girl, I reasoned, since her aunt had been so hospitable to me on my short stay in Canada.

In the spare room, so recently vacated by my mother, I quickly changed the bedding and began to unpack the holdall that was all Ashlyn had been carrying. Finding little more than jeans, T-shirts and some flimsy scraps of underwear, I put out a pair of my own warm pyjamas and a fleecy dressing gown and went to heat some soup.

Concentrating on what I was doing, I wasn't aware of her presence until a small sound made me turn to find Ashlyn standing in the doorway. She looked no more than a child with her face all scrubbed clean of make-up, and the fair hair curling to her slim shoulders. The dressing gown was too big and obviously far too long as she had to hold it up or she'd have tripped on the hem. She smiled at me and I told myself I would have had to be totally heartless not to have smiled back.

Ushering her towards the kitchen table, I said, 'I've phoned Jared to tell him you're safe. He was here earlier and I promised him I would let him know if you turned up.'

'He's here – in the UK?'

'Looking for you – yes. What did you think he would do when you took off without a word?'

'Urm,' she looked a bit sheepish and a guilty little smile played around lips that looked remarkably similar in shape to my own.

I didn't feel at all like smiling back this time. 'You didn't think at all. I'm right, aren't I?'

'I shouldn't have done that, right?'

'To be honest, it's not for me to tell you what to do, but don't you think your family has enough to deal with right now, without worrying about you and what you're up to.'

This time Ashlyn did have the decency to look a little shamefaced but also, I noticed, a bit defiant. Staring down into the now empty soup bowl, she mumbled, 'I had to do it now, or I was going to miss my chance.'

'Of a place at university?'

She looked up, at first obviously surprised, but then she hazarded, 'Jared told you, right?'

I nodded and then asked, 'Where have you applied?'

I was the one to be surprised when she said, 'Just here in Brankstone.'

'Why just the one, and why this one? Brankstone is a small and relatively new university compared to some of the others, as I told Jared. I'm sure with your qualifications and experience you could have had your pick.'

'But this is Dad's home town, the place I've heard about all of my life and I'd hoped – and so had Dad – that it was still the home of my sister. If I was living here we both knew there was a chance – however slim – of us meeting up, becoming a family. It's too late for Dad now, though he never gave up hope, you know, that you would get in touch – but it's not too late for us, is it?'

I wanted to say, there is no 'us,' and you are the last thing – the very last thing – I need in my life right now. I hadn't forgiven my father for walking away from me and to look every day at the replica daughter I'd so recently discovered he had created to take my place would be rubbing salt into a wound that had remained raw many years after an event that had been devastating for me.

I had opened my mouth to say the damning words, to advise her in the kindest terms that I could find that she had no place here in *my* country, but how could I when she was looking at me so hopefully with my father's eyes. I found even reminding myself crossly that I owed not a single thing to either one of them didn't help at all.

I compromised, just as I always seemed to do. 'I don't know,' I said feebly, 'you've had the advantage of growing up always knowing I existed and curiosity alone would make you want to get in touch. I'm afraid,' I said becoming braver, 'that I have no feelings for you one way or the other.'

I knew it was a lie even as the words left my mouth, but the feelings I had for Ashlyn were only childish ones of jealousy, rage and envy. As far as I was concerned, had my father not managed to create another family with the perfect two point four children in another country, he might have come looking for the child he'd left behind and – ridiculous as it may seem – I couldn't bring myself to forgive her for being born.

As young as she was I had the feeling Ashlyn realized all

of that, and I had to fight off the feelings of guilt that threatened to swamp me, reminding myself that I wasn't responsible for her welfare and certainly hadn't asked her to come here.

'You want me to leave, right?' It was a statement, said in the saddest tone, and she stood up, straightening her back, obviously trying her best to look dignified. I admired the effort against impossible odds, swamped as she was by the over-sized dressing gown.

'Where would you go at this time of night?' I asked bluntly, adding in what I recognized was a very grudging way, 'You can stay, for now. No doubt Jared will be along tomorrow and then you can sort out between you what happens next.' The inference was that it was their problem and definitely *not* mine.

I was glad to go to bed and try to sleep. The idea being to postpone thinking about all that had happened in a very short while. It was too much to take in. First the news of my father's whereabouts and his death, the rush to make it across to Canada in time for his memorial service and then the headlong dash back in order to confront my mother about her years of deceit. Then, before I could broach even one question there was the cancer scare to deal with, something that was on-going, and before I could get my head around any of that, I had a sister I never knew existed, prior to the trip to Canada, following me halfway round the world and landing on my doorstep. It was beginning to feel as if I was caught in the eye of a storm with bits of my past whirling around me.

Despite my exhausted state, sleep eluded me for hours.

When I did manage to doze off, I dreamed I was caught up in the middle of a growing family of hostile strangers who seemed determined to make me into one of them. Every time I tried to escape another shadowy figure barred my path until I was eventually caught and held by strong arms.

Feeling as if I was suffocating, I fought valiantly to gain my freedom. I woke to the sound of the phone ringing, rolled up in the duvet with the cat on top. The indignant look she gave me when I managed to dislodge her and shed the bedding would have been funny at another time or place.

Staggering into the hall, I was just in time to see Ashlyn reaching out for the receiver and my frantic, 'No-o-o-o-o-o-o,' failed to prevent her lifting the instrument to her ear and saying cheerfully, 'Hi, can I help you?'

'Your daughter?' Ashlyn looked around vaguely, and caught sight of me, arm outstretched, fingers clutching at thin air and mouthing, 'Give it to me.'

'Oh, yes,' she said helpfully, smiling sweetly at me, 'she's right here. Shall I pass you over. Me? Oh, I'm—'

I finally made it and snatching the phone away, said, 'Mum, how are you today?'

Refusing to be distracted she asked curiously, 'Who was that?'

'Oh, it's just a girl from upstairs. She popped by to borrow some sugar.'

Ashlyn was staring at me, and my mother went into disapproval mode as she recalled, 'I thought you told me a young man lived in the upstairs flat? Does he bring *girls* back to stay regularly?'

'It's one girl. He is over twenty-one, Mum, and he pays the mortgage. He's entitled to bring back whoever he likes – as am I, if I feel so inclined.'

'But you're married.'

'Divorced actually,' I reminded her firmly, and then quickly changing the subject, I asked again, 'How are you, anyway?'

This time she allowed herself to be distracted, and said, 'I feel fine. Well, to be honest I've never felt anything else. That's why Roy and I have decided this health scare is all something and nothing.'

Except that it wasn't for them to decide whether my mother was well or ill – that was what the tests were designed to find out and that was what I said, in no uncertain terms. The threat of cancer wasn't something you could safely ignore.

'Oh, don't fuss, Franny. I'll keep the appointment when it comes and have the biopsy too, if necessary, but I'm sure it will turn out to be a false alarm. Anyway, love, I did enjoy the shopping trip and Roy didn't say a word about how much I'd bought.'

I sincerely hoped this generous and supportive side of Roy's nature wasn't going to disappear as swiftly as it had appeared just because they had now managed to convince themselves that my mother's symptoms had been exaggerated. I also hoped with all my heart their optimism wasn't premature but, if it was, they both had to accept this wasn't something Roy could control by sheer force of will and that my mother's future care was better left to the experts. I had no doubt at all that Roy loved my mother with all of his heart but he didn't always know best, as difficult as that was for him to understand.

'Now, if you want me to come with you for any of the appointments, you only have to say,' I assured my mother, knowing that 'hanging around' was another of Roy's pet hates.

'But you have to go to work,' she protested.

'I've already explained that I don't "have to" do anything. I can always take time off for you.'

'I know where you are if I need you,' she said, adding belatedly, 'thank you – and thank you for your kindness over the last couple of days.'

I was quite touched by that. 'You're welcome, Mum,' I said and I meant it.'

'Why didn't you tell her who I am?' Ashlyn demanded the minute I had replaced the receiver, and then she looked at me suspiciously. 'She doesn't know about me, does she? Does she even know about my – our – Dad's death? Or any of it?'

'No,' I said simply.

'Why not? It's because she's ill, right? What's wrong with her?'

I'd had enough. 'That,' I said forcefully, 'has absolutely *nothing* to do with you, Ashlyn.' She looked taken aback at the tone I used, but I was past caring. 'I will deal with this – all of it – in my own way and my own good time and I will thank you not to interfere. Now, I am going for a shower – and I might be some time. Please do *not* answer the phone in my absence.'

I was determined not to rush. I needed to calm down and try to sort my head out. Too much had happened too quickly for my mind to take it in. The remnants of jet lag weren't helping at all and neither was having someone – an uninvited stranger – living in my space.

I took my time getting ready, straightening my hair, making my face up and choosing what I was going to wear carefully. Looking good always lifted my confidence levels and it gave me the feeling of being back in control. This was my life and it wasn't for anyone else to tell me how to live it. It had taken too long for me to realize that.

8

The long black sweater slid smoothly over hips that were still agreeably slim, settling over a dark grey skirt in a crinkly material, and then knee-length boots in black were added and a pretty bead necklace. The V-neck of the sweater was low enough to flatter my womanly curves, but not so low as to be indecent.

I straightened my back, smiled at my reflection and told myself I looked exactly what I was – a woman in control of her life.

The smile stayed in place until I walked into my kitchen and found Jared and his sister – I still refused to acknowledge her as mine – sitting at the table sipping tea.

Obviously, Ashlyn hadn't realized that my instruction not to answer the phone had also extended to the doorbell. I shuddered at the thought of the lengthy explanations that would have been expected if either my mother or Adrian had been standing on the step.

'Cup of tea?' Ashlyn offered brightly, adding, 'look I made it in the pot, just the way my Da ...' she hesitated and then went on, 'the way you do it in England.'

Jared was looking me up and down in a way I wasn't quite sure I liked, and I had to fight to stay calm and, in doing so, try to prevent the hot colour that threatened to flood my cheeks. I had a perfect right, I reminded myself crossly, to dress any way I damn well pleased, but I suddenly had the awful suspicion he thought I had dressed up for him.

'I didn't hear the doorbell,' I stated, just to make things clear, and looked reprovingly at Ashlyn who was carefully pouring tea into dainty cups that I never used. I found myself hoping they weren't dusty from sitting in the cupboard and then wondered why I cared.

She pushed the cup and saucer towards me, and it was a moment before she looked at me. 'I kind of guessed it would be Jared at the door, you know.'

'It might not have been,' I reproved frowning.

'Is there a problem?' Jared looked from one of us to the other, and Ashlyn shrugged helplessly.

'Only in so far as none of my family know that Ashlyn – or you either, are here.' A picture of Adrian's angry face when he stood on my doorstep the night before flashed into my mind, but ignoring it, I added, 'In fact, they don't know anything about you, and for the time being, I have reasons of my own for preferring it to stay that way.'

'Fran's mother is ill,' Ashlyn explained, 'and we're pretty sure she doesn't even know Dad died yet.'

'Thank you,' I said rather tartly, 'I can speak for myself.'

'You were coming home to talk to her …' Jared began.

'Yes, well, things don't always go according to plan, do they? I found out almost the minute I arrived home, that my mother might have breast cancer. She's currently undergoing tests and this is obviously not the best time to be tackling her about any issues I might have with her over the past.'

'Of course not and I'm really very sorry about your mother.' Jared didn't have to pretend that he was shocked – I could see it in his eyes. I wondered why my mother's illness would bother him so much and then I remembered the loss of his father – not to mention his stepfather – and knew he would certainly appreciate my current fears.

'Thank you for understanding.'

'You have enough to deal with right now and we should really get out from under your feet.' Jared drank the tiny cup of tea in one gulp, placed the cup carefully back onto the saucer and advised his sister, 'Get your things together.'

'Where are we going?' Ashlyn stared at him stupidly.

'Back to Canada, where else?'

She jumped up and the cup she had been holding dropped to the floor and smashed. 'No-o-o-o,' Ashlyn wailed, her eyes filling with tears that quickly spilled over onto her cheeks.

Watching her I wondered inconsequentially why it was that only very young women could cry and still manage to look beautiful.

'You can't stay here. Francesca already has quite enough on her plate, and you can't remain in a strange country all by yourself. Where will you live and what will you do for money?'

'I have money. You know I've been working between studying and that Dad will have provided for us all in his will. I can take care of myself.' Ashlyn's tone was defiant, but she sounded like a small and pretty frightened child.

Determined not to get involved in something that had nothing to do with me, I busied myself with the dustpan and brush and was tipping the shards of china into the bin when Jared lost his rag.

I jumped as he yelled, 'I don't want to hear another word. You're coming home with me, Ashlyn. This is not just about you, you know. We've all lost someone we loved dearly. Can you not think about someone apart from yourself for once? Think about your mother over there grieving and now in pieces over you going missing, too. Think about Francesca worrying about her mother on top of trying to come to terms with the death of a father she barely knew and the lifetime they spent apart – and think about me.'

Ashlyn stared at him, and muttered, 'You? What about you?'

'I lost Mitch, too, and you of all people knew how much he meant to me. Then there's his business, someone has to keep it running, and until we know his exact wishes that someone has to be me. There is no one else and he would have trusted me to pick up the reigns – and I cannot do that from England.'

Ashlyn was silent for a moment and I thought perhaps the enormity of what she had done was finally coming home to her. If I thought she was going to meekly do Jared's bidding, though, I couldn't have been more wrong.

'They might already have my application at Brankstone University and be considering me for a place on the social work course,' she pointed out, obviously unwilling to give up without some sort of fight.

Jared looked as if he might be about to blow a gasket for

the second time, so I nipped in smartly to say, 'Well, there's one way to find out. Give them a ring and find out.'

When Ashlyn had taken herself and the phone off into the sitting room, I took the time to explain to Jared, 'There are deadlines for applications and Ashlyn has missed the first one, which was in January. Late applications are rarely considered for popular courses like social work, so I think you can safely say you will both soon be on your way home.'

Jared's clear relief was short-lived, and I was left feeling extremely foolish when Ashlyn burst into the room waving the phone about and yelling, 'They have my application and they're interested, you know. They want to invite me for an interview.'

'Just like that?' I asked, when Jared seemed at a loss for words.

'The lady I spoke to said something about a shortfall and considering late applications because of it. She's shortlisted my application and said she was very impressed with my experience. Kathryn Horne, she said her name was. She sounded lovely on the phone and was ever so helpful, especially when I told her about Dad.

'I have to fill in a supplementary form, which she has already emailed to me, and get it back to her ASAP. They are just in the process of arranging additional interview dates and as soon as she gets my completed form she will get back to me. The fact that I'm already in the UK makes it all so much simpler, she said.'

There was a deafening silence, and then she said, very quietly, 'Please don't make me go home, Jared, not without at least trying to see if I can get a place.'

Jared was at a complete loss and in spite of myself I felt sorry for him. In fact, I felt sorry for us all, feeling that this crazy situation was of Mitchell Browning's making – he'd encouraged the girl to come to the UK after all – and he wasn't even around to sort it out.

I heard myself saying the words, even though I couldn't quite believe they were coming out of my mouth. I sounded resigned and I knew that I was, but even as I spoke I was wondering why on earth I was making this into my problem. 'Ashlyn can stay with me – just for the time being.'

Screaming loud enough to burst my eardrums she threw herself at me, calming down enough eventually to assure me, 'You won't regret this, Fran,' but I knew that I already did. I couldn't think when I had regretted anything more, actually, especially when she continued, 'You can't make me go home now, Jared. You know that I'll be quite safe living with my own sister.'

'Are you quite sure about this, Francesca?' He was frowning.

'I only meant it as a temporary measure,' I hastened to point out, 'just until the interview.' I tried not to hope that the resulting decision would be an unsuccessful one for Ashlyn, but knew it would solve a lot of problems if that were the outcome.

'What will you tell your mother?' Jared asked above Ashlyn shrieking round the kitchen like a child high on E numbers.

'Probably that she's a student from the university. That's about as close as I can get to the truth and I will use the same story for anyone else who calls just to keep things simple.'

'I hope you won't regret making this generous offer,' he said quietly, adding with a straight look at me, 'if you haven't already.' He shook his head and then put out a hand to stop Ashlyn in her tracks. 'Didn't you say something about completing a form? Why don't you ask Francesca if you can use her laptop to log on and download it – no time like the present.'

'Thank you – thank you both, you're the best brother and sister in the world,' Ashlyn said effusively 'and I'll do everything I can to repay you. I'll be the best student social worker that Brankstone University has ever seen.'

'First things first,' I reminded her, 'you have a form to fill in.'

I left her hunched over the laptop in the sitting room and went back into the kitchen to find that Jared had made a fresh pot of tea and found the mugs. He started pouring as soon as I walked in.

I sat down and wrapped my hands around the mug he set in front of me, needing the warmth.

'You feel as if you've been run over by a truck, right?' he asked with sympathy in his tone.

I nodded, 'Mmm, is she always like that?'

'Exuberant, excitable, intent on getting her own way at any price?' Jared nodded back. 'I'm afraid so. You're beginning to realize what you've taken on, right? I thought so, she's a typical headstrong teenager, but she does have redeeming traits, too. Ashlyn can be very sweet and loving, she'd do anything for anyone, and is generous to a fault.

She's not afraid of hard work and I think she will make a great social worker.'

'You think she will get the place, then?'

'Don't you?'

'I'm amazed they still have places, because I've temped at the university and I know it's one of the courses that is always very over subscribed. There will be other excellent candidates, perhaps older and with more experience.'

'Well, Ashlyn will at least get her chance, thanks to you. It was very good of you to offer to put her up, because I'm quite certain it was the very last thing you wanted. What made you relent?'

'I can't even begin to tell you,' I said, and I couldn't.

It had taken me years to get my life just the way I wanted it, with no one else to consider, no one to answer to. I loved having my home to myself and now I had opened the door to probably the very last person I would have chosen to share it with.

'How do you think your mother will take it?' I wondered out loud.

'I think she will come round to the idea, especially as Ashlyn has you to watch out for her and, as you've already said, it's not a foregone conclusion that she will even get a place. I guess for now we will have to wait and see.'

The form was eventually completed to Ashlyn's satisfaction and emailed back to the recruitment administrator dealing with the course, the same woman she had spoken to earlier. After a sandwich lunch, I offered to drive us all over to the university, just to take a look at it from the outside, and suggested finishing with a quick tour of the area.

'Just to give you an idea of where you would be living – if you do gain a place.' I quickly added the warning, 'It's hardly London with all its shops, theatres and the bright lights, but the students seem to manage to entertain themselves adequately with what is on offer. You would also be kept very busy with coursework and placements.'

Squeezed into my ancient VW Beetle we looked like the typical family unit that we certainly were not and, I realized with dismay, Jared and I might easily be mistaken for Ashlyn's parents. How very weird was that?

Ashlyn insisted on sitting in the back, and ooh-ed and ah-ed her way around the town, pointing out this and that with much more enthusiasm that the area really deserved.

It made me wonder, looking around with my usual jaundiced eye, why I hadn't considered moving away and starting a new life elsewhere – especially since my divorce. I kept telling myself I was as free as a bird and yet I'd made no effort whatever to spread my wings.

I'd always convinced myself I'd stayed put because of my mother, but the truth was she lived abroad for several months of the year and hadn't really needed me at all until the recent turn of events. We'd never had what I imagined was a typical mother and daughter relationship. Far from always being on the phone sharing girlie chats, neither of us made much effort at all to keep in touch and that was the way it had always been.

I could pretend otherwise all I wanted, and usually did, but deep down inside I knew the reason I hadn't moved away was so that my father would be able to find me if he ever came looking. That he never had, had always been tremendously hard for me to accept, but since my trip to Canada, I was left wondering if that really was his choice – or if it was my mother's decision to keep him out of my life – and whether I would ever find answers to those and all the other questions that had plagued me for almost the whole of my life.

9

'It's the very least I can do, after everything you've done and will be doing for Ashlyn.'

To my discomfort Jared was insisting on setting up a direct debit to pay for Ashlyn's keep while she was staying with me, overriding all of my objections, and refusing to take no for an answer to that or the celebration meal he wanted us to share.

Ashlyn clapped her hands. 'Our first real family meal together.'

I was equally insistent that none of it was necessary, but was obviously fighting a losing battle against the two of them and aware that I was beginning to look ungrateful into the bargain. I wondered if the bloody family always got its own way, but didn't intend to give up without at least the appearance of a struggle.

'You have a flight to get first thing in the morning,' I pointed out, thinking longingly of cheese on toast and an early night though, in my heart I knew it was only a matter of time before I conceded defeat.

Increasingly, it seemed as if my life was being taken over,

beginning with the phone call from Julie advising me of my father's death. These days I never got over one crisis before another one loomed. I felt as if I was being put through a wringer and hung out to dry as one thing after another was thrown at me. What I wanted above anything was some quiet time to mull things over but I had a strong feeling my quiet times were well and truly over.

I gave in eventually, of course, just as I knew I would. That's all I had been doing of late. My better judgement seemed to well and truly have deserted me. I was a grown woman and yet I seemed to have reverted to the timid girl who went along with everyone else's decisions for a quiet life.

When my mother had refused to discuss my father's reasons for leaving I had never insisted on my right to know what those reasons were – not even when I was grown up – just as I had never insisted Adrian and I discuss our fertility and subsequent marriage problems. Perhaps, in my insecurity, I had been afraid they would leave me if I did and yet, in the end, it was I who had distanced myself from them.

'We could send out for a takeaway,' I made one last stab at what I thought was an acceptable compromise.

'No,' they were both shaking their heads.

'Take us somewhere typically English,' Jared suggested, 'but it had better not be too dressy because I would put money on Ashlyn only packing jeans in her luggage.'

I threw my hands up. 'Oh, go on then. I give in. Do you *always* get your own way?' I laughed in spite of myself, 'No, don't bother to answer that. I don't really want to know.'

We went to the local Toby Carvery – cheap and cheerful, but good food and plenty of it. I noticed that both Jared and Ashlyn heaped their plates and were tucking into the roasted meat and vegetables with every appearance of enjoyment. They were certainly going out of their way to be entertaining and seemed in exceptionally good spirits. Common sense told me it was because Ashlyn had got her own way and Jared's problem of what to do about her had been solved, but I had to admit it was the most I had enjoyed myself in a very long time. I wondered if, against my better judgement, I was allowing them both to slip under my normal strenuous guard and felt a little shudder of unease.

'Oh, very cosy.'

I hadn't seen him come in the restaurant, but suddenly Adrian was approaching our table with a supercilious sneer all over his normally placid face. All done up in his usual work garb of white shirt, dark suit and tie, my first thought was that he looked stuffy and overdressed compared to Jared, who wore black jeans, T-shirt and leather jacket.

I smiled, refusing to let his sudden appearance rile me. 'Hello, Adrian, how are you? Let me introduce you to some friends of mine. Ashlyn, Jared, this is Adrian.'

Jared immediately rose to his feet and held out a hand – which Adrian rudely ignored – and said, 'Nice to meet you. Any friend of Francesca's is a friend—'

'I'm not a friend, I'm her *husband*,' Adrian said with heavy emphasis, and then repeated himself in a louder tone for Ashlyn and Jared's benefit, obviously in case they hadn't heard clearly the first time, 'her *husband*.'

'Adrian is, in fact, my ex-husband,' I corrected firmly and rather waspishly, 'and we have been divorced for some time. Now, is there something I can help you with, Adrian? Only we are trying to finish our meal.' I looked around curiously, 'Are you here with someone, because they'll be wondering where you've got to, won't they?'

My first instinct had been to demand what the hell he thought he was playing at, but keeping cool had been a good move on my part, I soon realized. Watching him struggle with what was a very reasonable query, a suspicion suddenly popped into my mind and had to be dealt with.

'You haven't followed me here, have you?'

'No, of course not.' His denial was too swift to be convincing and he flushed a deep and very unbecoming red to the roots of his floppy fair hair.

'You have, haven't you? Just what the hell do you think you're playing at?' I demanded furiously, careful not to raise my voice. I stood up, and asked Ashlyn and Jared to, 'Excuse us for one moment, would you?' and seizing Adrian by the elbow I forced him towards the entrance and out into the car park.

'Well?' I stood with my hands on my hips. 'I'm waiting, Adrian, and this has better be good.'

'I still care for you, Franny. I just wanted to make sure you were okay,' he excused, and it took me all my time not to scream my frustration in his face.

'No. No, you didn't. This isn't about caring – it's never about caring with you. This is about control, Adrian, just as it always has been. But it stops, right here, right now. It's over. We're over.'

'No.' He looked anguished, and in spite of myself, I did feel sorry for him.

Suddenly mindful of my dinner companions, I knew I had to get rid of him, at least for now, or I would be standing there all night.

'Go home,' I told him. 'We can talk about this some other time, but not now. I must get back to my friends.'

'Oh, yes,' he said and the sneer was back on his face, 'your friends.'

'Stop it right now,' I ordered, 'or I promise I will put you right out of my life for good.'

Adrian's expression changed. 'You can't do that, I'm your husband.'

'I can and I will, if this doesn't stop, and you are *not* my husband. Now go home.'

'You said we can talk some other time,' he reminded me, and to hasten his departure, I said rashly, 'I'll ring you and arrange something.'

'When? Tomorrow?'

God, he grew more and more like a persistent child. 'Yes, tomorrow.'

When I got back to Ashlyn and Jared, I was horrified to find they'd been waiting for me to come back before getting on with their meal.

'It will be stone cold,' I protested.

'I was finished anyway,' Ashlyn insisted and then asked, 'I didn't realize you'd been married. Is he always like that?'

'Unfortunately, yes.' I pulled a rueful face. 'If anything I think he's actually got worse with age.'

'I guess he's not the one who wanted the divorce, huh?' Jared looked serious. 'Does he follow you around a lot?'

I shook my head and forked a piece of roast potato into my mouth. It had been delicious before, but now it was cold and unappetizing and I chewed without enthusiasm. 'Just phone calls mainly. You know the sort of thing, "Just checking to see you're all right," which is kind but can get a bit wearing. I thought we could be adult about the split and it would be easier if we could remain friends. Perhaps it wasn't such a great idea after all, and I'm just allowing him false hopes of a reconciliation that is never going to happen.'

Jared nodded, 'Something like that always works better in theory than it does in fact, right?'

'Mmm. I'm afraid you might be right. Anyway, he's gone now, so can we talk about something else and perhaps order a delicious pudding each.'

'Great idea.' Ashlyn greeted the suggestion with enthusiasm and spent an age pouring over the menu choices, declaring, 'There are so many things I haven't tried, I don't even know where to start.'

'Choose your favourite,' I advised, 'and we can always come back again so that you can try something else.'

'Or you could just order two and hurry things along,' Jared suggested, and we all laughed and made our choices.

I put all thoughts of Adrian out of my mind for another time. There was a moment, on my way back from the ladies with Ashlyn, when I felt almost certain I'd caught a glimpse of Adrian, or someone who looked very like him, standing among the crowd at the bar, but when I looked again he had gone and I convinced myself I had imagined it.

Jared didn't come in when we got back to my flat, but he enveloped Ashlyn in a bear hug and reminded her, quite forcefully, how much she owed me and not on any account to abuse my hospitality.

'I will be phoning to check from time to time,' he said, before kissing her soundly and telling her that he loved her very much and wished her luck with her application. 'Let me know when the interview date comes through.'

He then turned his attention to me and, ignoring the hand I held out, he wrapped me into his arms and held me so close I swear you wouldn't have got a tissue between us.

Coming from an undemonstrative family, and married for years to a man who was great at control but rubbish at cuddles, my first instinct was to pull away. My second was to enjoy the novelty of just being held and the feeling of strong male arms around me. I almost whimpered when he put me away to then hold me at arms' length so that he could look into my face.

'We'll never be able to thank you, you know,' he said, all signs of laughter erased from his face and his eyes. 'I know this whole situation isn't of your choosing. You've been left with little choice but to get involved, and yet you've come through for us in a way I could never have imagined. You might have noticed I had my doubts about you when we first met.'

'You don't say,' I said, with a liberal measure of sarcasm I found easier to produce now that there was a bit of distance between us. 'I never would have guessed.'

'It was that obvious, right?'

'You can say that again – with feeling.'

'I'm sorry.' Jared put a finger under my chin and tilted my face until he was looking directly into my eyes. I suppressed a shiver, but whether it was from cold, excitement, fear or something else entirely, I had no idea. 'I admit I've never been more wrong about a person. I wasn't at all sure about you to start with, but you're a real lady and if you ever decide you do want to be part of our family, I know I speak for us all when I say we would be honoured and privileged to have you.'

In spite of myself, and my determination to keep my father's replacement family at arms' length – whatever circumstances we found ourselves in – I couldn't help but be touched. I suspected that admitting he was wrong was not something that Jared did very often. Even so, the about turn on his part wasn't anywhere near enough to make me want to keep them in my life or to make a more permanent and tangible relationship with them. When I thought back to the peace of my life before I knew they existed it was with an overwhelming feeling of longing.

'Thank you,' I said, and I almost meant it. I even let him embrace me again, though I made no attempt to hug him back, keeping my arms pinned to my sides.

'He's great, isn't he?' Ashlyn stated when we'd waved Jared off in a taxi and had closed the front door behind us.

I wasn't going to agree, but it seemed a bit unfeeling to upset her this early on by disagreeing, so I countered with another question. 'You're very fond of Jared, aren't you?'

She looked at me in surprise. 'Oh, yes, why wouldn't I be?'

'I don't know, do I?' I shrugged, 'I've never had a brother.'

'Or a sister,' she reminded me, adding excitedly, 'until now.' Looking at me with pleading puppy dog eyes, she was obviously willing me to be thrilled.

People pleaser that I was I just couldn't bring myself to let her down and I agreed weakly, 'Until now.'

Obviously eager to please herself, Ashlyn fussed around for what was left of the evening, offering tea, coffee, hot chocolate, even a hot water bottle for my bed as if I were her maiden aunt instead of her sister.

It took a minute or two before I realized with a start that I'd actually acknowledged the relationship between us for the first time. Scowling I reminded myself that it didn't mean I was ready to start playing happy families with the girl. I had offered Ashlyn a roof over her head for a very short period of time – just until she was either rejected or accepted onto the course of her choice. If it were the former, she would very soon be on her way back to Canada; if the latter, she could move into student accommodation and live her own life – on her own – and leave me to mine.

I suddenly found myself getting really quite angry at the situation I found myself in but, eventually, without too much thought, even I had to accept that it was almost entirely of my own making. What on earth I had been thinking to invite the girl into my home in the first place, I had no idea, but to then invite her to stay on for an indefinite period had been an act of pure madness.

Over the next few days it increasingly irritated me that Ashlyn had already made herself right at home – even though I knew I had clearly indicated that she should. She hadn't brought much with her but what she did have seemed to be spread all around the flat. A pair of shoes here, a lip gloss there, and Ashlyn herself seemed to be permanently sprawled the length of my couch with her head in some American soap on TV, so that I was relegated to an armchair that I rarely used and didn't much like.

I was biting my tongue so often that it was a wonder it was still intact and attached, and my ill humour wasn't helped by yet another phone call from Adrian badgering me to meet up with the reminder, 'You promised.' In the end I agreed because it would get me out of the house, though an evening of Adrian's company was no more appealing than an evening downgraded to the armchair in the company of Ashlyn.

I needed, I decided, as I left the house – leaving Ashlyn and the disloyal Ellie cosied up together on the couch watching *ER* – to be much more firm with the pair of them. It was my home, my life, and it was entirely up to me to make that much clearer to the pair of them.

It was in this frame of mind that I walked into the local pub ten minutes early for our meeting to find Adrian already waiting. He leapt to his feet the minute he saw me, almost tripping over in his eagerness to help me off with my coat.

'I've already bought your sherry, dry, just as you like it.'

I made my first stand. 'I don't know whatever gave you the idea that I like sherry, Adrian. I prefer vodka and tonic.'

He looked as shocked as if I'd said I'd just taken up a job lap-dancing. 'But you always said you liked sherry.'

'No,' I pointed out. 'I drank it once at a funeral, many years ago, and *you* decided that I liked it. I just drank it because it didn't seem worth making a fuss. I've always preferred vodka and tonic, actually.' I left him sitting with his mouth open and bought my own drink with a great feeling of satisfaction.

'Now,' I took the seat across the table from him, 'what did you want to talk to me about, because to be honest I'm not sure what else there is left to be said. As far as I'm concerned we said everything there was to say before the divorce.'

'I still don't understand how or why it happened.'

I bit back the word, 'tough,' and felt for my poor mangled tongue. I realized, though Adrian obviously didn't, that he didn't understand because he simply didn't listen and this was confirmed by his next words.

'I thought we were happy.'

'I wasn't,' I said simply, 'and I'm sorry if it offends you to hear me say that. We'd lived apart for the required time and the papers were signed by each of us. We both agreed our marriage was over.'

'I didn't.'

'You've left it a little late to bring it up. The divorce was finalized some time ago,' I pointed out, quite kindly but with growing impatience.

'I never thought you would actually go through with it, I thought that you would come to your senses.'

I refrained from asking if he had ever listened to a single word I'd said, since it was patently obvious he had not and, I realized belatedly, I must take some of the blame for that. I should have been more insistent, should have *made* myself heard, but could only wonder if it would have made any difference in the end if I had.

I sighed deeply and changed the subject. 'There's no point going over old ground. What's done is done. What did you want to talk about, Adrian?'

'I wondered if I could move in with you – just for a while?'

10

I was taking a sip of my drink as Adrian made his outrageous request, in the most reasonable tone of voice. The shock of his words caused an involuntary jerk of my elbow and made the sip become more of a gulp, which immediately went down the wrong way. I choked, coughed and battled to get air into my labouring lungs.

Eyes streaming, I gasped, 'Move in with me? Are you quite mad?'

He patted my back ineffectually, asked, 'Are you all right?' and added, 'It would only be for a short time,' as if that made everything all right.

'Why?' It was all I could think of to say, apart from, 'Over my dead body,' which seemed a bit harsh, even if it was true.

'Subsidence.' Adrian drew the word out with a grand flourish and there was a pleased expression on his face that he wasn't quite able to hide. 'Have to get the builders in. I just couldn't stand the mess and the noise and so I thought....'

Oh, yes, I knew exactly what he thought. I was as sure as I could be that you couldn't invent subsidence, but Adrian had quite obviously instantly seen it as an opportunity he could use to his own advantage. He had never accepted that our marriage was over and this was the perfect excuse for him to get his feet under my table on a day-to-day basis.

I shuddered and wasted a moment or two thrashing around looking for a valid excuse for my refusal, while he looked at me with an 'it's the least you can do' expression on his face. I cursed my inability to give a straight no, realizing it came from a ridiculous sense of guilt I still carried over our divorce.

Then it came to me in a flash of enlightenment, the revelation that I could say no with a squeaky clean conscience. I had the perfect excuse sprawled out on my sofa at home and in that moment I felt suddenly very – well, *quite* – fond of Ashlyn.

I pulled my face into what I felt was a suitably regretful look and said, 'Oh, I'm sorry, Adrian. I just don't have the room.'

'You have a *spare room*, Francesca.' I noticed his tone had become quite hard and forceful. I recognized it from all the times in our marriage when it didn't look as if he was going to get his own way. Adrian liked to give the impression of being mild and easy going, but there was a thread of steel to his attitude when his wishes looked likely to be thwarted. 'Your mother stayed in it only recently.'

'That's right,' I agreed, with a smile, 'and now I have another guest sleeping in there.'

He didn't even try to hide the look of pure fury that darkened his face and narrowed his eyes. 'Well,' he drawled, 'the guy from the other night, I presume. How very convenient. Are you sure he's in the *spare* room?'

My fingers itched to slap his sneering face – hard – and I held onto my temper with difficulty. 'No,' I said, 'not him, the girl from the other night. I'd like to say it's not like you to jump to wrong conclusions, but that was just one of the problems in our marriage, wasn't it, Adrian? I've lost count of the number of things I've been falsely accused of over the years and the embarrassment that has often caused us both.'

'If you're referring to the incident with your boss, I did explain at the time.' He shifted uncomfortably in his chair.

'So you did,' I said, thinking back to just one of many scenes he had caused when he thought, as he'd always put it, 'something was going on.'

Adrian changed the subject quickly, something else he frequently did when he didn't like the way the conversation was going. 'Well, how long is she going to be there? A few days at most, I expect. I can put the builders off and move in after that.'

The audacity of the man took my breath away. 'I decided to take a student in,' I began, which wasn't so very far from the truth, 'for the money and the company,' which was. 'Ashlyn will be with me for the three year duration of her course.' I only just refrained from adding, so there.

Adrian looked affronted. 'If it's money you need you should have spoken to me, and you always told me you liked your own company.'

'It's not your money I need, and I have my own life now which means I can enjoy the company of others – or not – as it pleases me.' I gave him a straight look, which he obviously interpreted correctly.

'I didn't stop you having friends.'

But we both knew he had made the majority of visitors to our home feel most unwelcome and he'd never even tried to be subtle about it. Putting out milk bottles and winding up a bedside alarm clock in front of your guests was a pretty big hint that you expected them to leave.

Within a few years of our wedding I had given up even trying to have a social life, it had just been easier to do what Adrian wanted. At least that way I got the quiet life I began to crave and an agreeable husband – because he was much easier to live with once he got his own way.

'All water under the bridge now, isn't it?' I finished my drink with no further mishap and reached for my handbag. 'So if that was all. I'm sorry I can't help out, but you can see how it is. Perhaps you can rent somewhere.'

'Stay,' he said, suddenly, putting his hand on top of mine. I stared pointedly at his hand and then at his face. He flushed, looked as if he was going to have something to say, thought better of it, and took his hand away. 'Please?' he pleaded. 'I really would like us to be friends.'

'Yes,' I agreed, 'I would have preferred that, but it doesn't appear to be working very well. I left our marriage because I needed room to breathe. I couldn't move for you then and it sometimes feels as if nothing has changed.'

'It's only because I—'

'Care?' I nodded, 'Yes, you've told me so many times, but there's a subtle difference between caring for someone and suffocating them. I'm a big girl now and I really can manage on my own, you know.'

'You couldn't when you went away,' he reminded me sulkily. 'You had no one you could ask to feed the cat.'

'Yes, thank you for reminding me,' I said coolly, assuring myself I would get Ellie a pet passport and take her with me or put her in a cattery before I would ever depend on his help again. 'It was a bit of an emergency, but I'm sure the guy upstairs would have done it if I'd thought to ask him.'

The familiar sneer was back in a minute, 'Oh, yes, I just *bet* he would,' he said with a knowing look. 'Do anything for you, would he?'

'That's it,' I reached for my handbag again and practically snatched it up. 'That's quite enough. I know exactly what you are insinuating in your usual not very subtle way and I will not put up with your snide comments for another minute. You just never learn, do you? That's why we are no longer married, Adrian, and also why I no longer have to put up with it.'

'I'm sorry.'

'Yes,' I sighed deeply, 'you always are. The fact remains that we can't go on like this with you thinking you can still control me, deciding who I can and cannot see, ringing all the time and turning up on my doorstep whenever it suits you. *If* we're to remain friends we have to set a few ground rules because at the moment, let me tell you, you are skating on very thin ice.'

He looked mutinous and as if there was quite a lot he wanted to say, but he must have guessed he would have found himself sitting on his own with no way back into my life, so limited himself to a pithy, 'Such as?'

'Such as turning up at my home *only* when you're invited, such as rationing your phone calls to one a week, if that, and such as finding a social life of your own instead of constantly checking up on mine and making assumptions you have no business to be making about the people I know. How I spend my time and who with is nothing to do with you. Is that clear? I do *not* have to ask your permission to have dinner with friends and to have you turn up and insult them is absolutely *not* bloody well acceptable.'

'I didn't.'

'Yes,' I said, 'you did, and I will not have it.'

It took me all my time to extract even a half-hearted promise from Adrian and I was very aware he simply couldn't see that his constantly hassling me was out of order.

I'd thought that our separation and subsequent divorce was going to set me free. Walking the short distance home and enjoying the warm evening air and the solitude, I could finally see that in trying to keep everything amicable I had simply encouraged Adrian to believe our relationship wasn't really over.

I had to fight the urge to peer over my shoulder to see if he was following me. I wouldn't have put it past him. In fact, I was beginning to think I wouldn't put anything past him and there was no doubt in my mind that I must get tougher with him – much tougher – or the life I had dreamed of would never be mine.

'Are you sure you don't want a lift? It looks like rain to me.'

I jumped as the car drew silently up beside me, and yelled furiously, 'Jesus, Adrian, don't creep up on me like that. Didn't you listen to a word I said back there? No, I don't want a bloody lift. What I want is for you to leave me alone.'

I was a bundle of nerves by the time I reached home and

I almost screamed as my upstairs neighbour came in the gate almost immediately behind me.

I must have made a sound, because he said, 'Oh, sorry, did I startle you? I can't say we'll have to stop meeting like this, because we never do, do we? Amazing really, with us living so close and using the same entrance.'

Pulling myself together with an effort, I made a feeble attempt at a joke, 'Obviously we're both great housekeepers,' and then seeing his puzzled look I elaborated, 'because we never run out of coffee, sugar or soap powder.'

'Oh, yeah, right.' He grinned and reminded me, 'It would be a poor excuse, though, with a corner shop a stone's throw away. Your cat, is it?' he nodded towards Ellie who had appeared to wind herself round our legs. 'She sometimes pops up to see me.'

'Oh, I hope she isn't making a nuisance of herself.' I bent to stroke her head and when I straightened up we were suddenly face to face and so close I could see the startling blue of his eyes and note that the stubble on his chin was almost the same length as that on his cropped head.

He must have noticed me looking because he ran a self-conscious hand across his head. 'I keep it short because I'm a builder. It gets too hot and too messy if I try to grow it and, anyway, it's *curly*,' he said in such a disgusted tone that I burst out laughing.

'You obviously don't have that trouble.' He reached out a hand as if he was going to touch my smooth hair, but pulled it back even before I had the chance to duck away.

'Actually,' I smiled up at him, liking what I saw and wondering why I hadn't paid any attention to my upstairs neighbour before, 'I spend half my life straightening mine since I don't have the option of shaving it off.'

He laughed out loud, and put out his hand. 'Lloyd,' he said.

'Francesca – Fran,' I replied, putting my hand into a grip that was a little rough, probably from the kind of work he did, and pleasantly strong.

'Nice to meet you.'

'Likewise,' I said, and let myself in, calling the cat in behind me as Lloyd carried on around the side of the house to his own front door.

Ashlyn must have been listening out for me because the door wasn't even closed behind me before she called from the direction of the kitchen, 'I've just put the kettle on, can I make you a drink?'

That was an offer you didn't get when you lived alone, I thought, still feeling mellow towards her for being my water-tight reason for keeping Adrian out of my spare room.

'Cup of tea would be lovely,' I called back.

'I thought you'd say that, so I've already warmed the pot. Who were you talking to?'

I hung my jacket on the hook in the hall and said as I walked into the kitchen, 'Just my upstairs neighbour.'

'Mmm, quite nice, isn't he? Rugged. About your age, right?' Before I had the chance to wonder just what she was hinting at, Ashlyn went on, 'I thought perhaps your ex had given you a lift home.'

I gritted my teeth not wanting to speak or even think about Adrian. 'No,' I said shortly, 'I walked.'

We sat at the kitchen table, quite companionably, and sipped our tea.

'I've told the agency I'll be going back to work next week,' I commented, 'so you'll have to get used to your own company. It must be quiet for you here after being with your family.'

'There was always a houseful at home.' Ashlyn nodded and then added in a confidential tone that was little more than a whisper, though there was no one to hear, 'Sometimes I almost wished I was an only child, or that it was just me and Jared, which is pretty selfish of me, right? Given all the good work my Mom and Dad did with disadvantaged kids.'

If I was surprised by her words I thought I hid it well and merely said, 'Being an only child is not all it's cracked up to be and you can take that from one who knows. It can be pretty lonely and I never did make friends easily, even as a child.'

'Oh,' Ashlyn looked at me over the rim of her mug. It was my favourite cat one and I noticed she used it all the time, and that my only cat was sitting on her lap right at that minute. In a very short time she seemed to have made herself right at home. 'I did wonder,' she said carefully, adding, 'I know I haven't been here long but I couldn't help noticing that no one ever pops by.'

'It's a long story,' I told her, refusing to elaborate, 'and I'm off to bed. Goodnight.'

'Fran?'

I turned around to look at her and Ashlyn smiled before assuring me, 'Now that I'm here you'll never be lonely again.'

11

It seemed as if Ashlyn was determined to prove herself right because she never gave me a moment alone until I went to bed at night. It was almost a relief to return to work because, as a temp, I never really got to know my colleagues well. Although most were friendly enough, they knew I wouldn't be there long and so made little attempt to invade either my privacy or my space.

Whenever they talked about family or their social lives I always kept my head down and got on with my work. It wasn't all down to Adrian; I had always preferred to keep my private life private. I'd probably been that way ever since someone at school had found it hilarious that I had no father and told me I must be a little bastard. It didn't take much for the other kids to jump on the bandwagon and taunt me mercilessly. The humiliation had never left me; even after all these years I cringed whenever I thought about it.

I wasn't even old enough then to know what the term meant, but was old enough to understand that my mother wouldn't like it. It was years before I discovered what 'bastard' actually meant, that it wasn't even strictly true, and the girl must have been even more ignorant than I was. Even so, I still didn't want to take the chance on anything like that ever happening again, so my family circumstances became a carefully guarded secret and yet another reason why I found it so hard to make friends.

Ashlyn didn't seem to have that problem, and appeared to spend the hours not sprawled on the couch in front of the TV getting on first name terms with neighbours I had never shared the time of day with. I was amazed how much she knew about them all but discouraged the sharing of details, feigning disinterest. It was a relief when, within a few days, she met me at the door with the news that her interview date had come though.

'Kathryn – you know, Mrs Horne the recruitment lady – phoned to say there has been a cancellation next Monday and I could have that slot. That was really nice of her, right?'

I agreed, and wondered if this would be the end of it. There must be far more applicants for the social work course than there were places and I was sure I had heard somewhere that they preferred older applicants because they generally had more experience. The chance of Ashlyn getting in had to be minimal. Once the 'unsuccessful' decision had been made through UCAS she would surely give up on the idea of studying in England and go home.

The whole point of her making an application to Brankstone in the first place – if what she had said originally was true – was so that she could find me for Mitchell. Well, now she knew where I was, Mitchell was dead and she had surely realized by now that any sort of a close relationship between us was out of the question, given what a mismatched pair we were.

I tried to match her enthusiastic tone. 'You've phoned your Mum and told her the good news – and Jared, of course?'

'Well, no, I wanted to tell you first.'

I was surprised by how touched I was by that simple statement – when what I really wanted was to be irritated because she was insisting on treating me like family when we were still very far from that.

'Do it now,' I insisted, picking up the house phone that I was pretty sure she'd never yet made use of, 'on this.'

'It costs a lot in England, though, to phone overseas, right?' she hesitated, looking doubtful.

'It's fine. I think I can afford it. Save running up your mobile bill.'

The call was so lengthy that I began to regret my generosity. She sounded so young and so excited, sharing her news with her family, and I felt sad that I couldn't ever remember feeling that young or that excited. Then she insisted on handing the phone to me and I had a conversation that was friendly enough but still very stilted, with the woman my father had chosen to create another family with to replace the one he left behind.

When I spoke to Jared he was, like his mother, very grateful for the hospitality I was showing to Ashlyn. 'And you,' he said, 'how are you? Any more problems with the ex?'

'Why would you think that?'

'Well, I know I only met the guy once but he seemed a bit – obsessed.'

I smiled in spite of myself, pleased that someone agreed

with me. 'He thinks he's being caring. He likes to give that impression.'

'Creepy is the word I would use.'

'Oh,' I dismissed easily, 'I think I can handle Adrian.'

'I hope so. I worry about you – both.'

I was quite enjoying his concern and his caring tone and then realized with a pang that I was being foolish and it was all for his sister. Which, of course, I reminded myself sharply, was exactly as it should be.

He tried to talk about money, as had Cheryl, but I again dismissed the direct debit offer with the reminder that it had only been for a short time. They could do nothing about it without the bank details that I had so far refused to share.

'But if Ashlyn gets the offer of a place and the arrangement becomes more permanent, we'll have to have a proper discussion.'

Over my dead body would it become a permanent arrangement; I had already made my mind up about that, but I merely made a non-committal, 'Mmmm'.

Before Jared hung up, he assured me he would get over to the UK again as soon as he could and that he would ring on Monday to see how the interview went. 'I don't want Ashlyn running up your phone bill the way she does Mom's,' he said dryly, 'and I hope she's behaving herself.'

I could hardly say she rarely moved from the couch except to gossip with the neighbours occasionally, and merely commented, 'She's no trouble, really.'

'I'm glad to hear it.'

Passing the phone back to Ashlyn, I left her to say her goodbyes and wandered into the kitchen with the idea of putting together a quick meal. I was poking about in the fridge when I heard the phone ring again and straightened up just in time to have the instrument thrust into my hand.

'Who on earth have you been on the phone to all this time?'

For a moment I thought it was Adrian and I was just about to tell him sharply to mind his own bloody business, when I realized the voice wasn't quite right – although it was familiar.

'I've been trying to get through for ages. Your mother's very upset.'

The penny dropped, and I said quickly, 'What's the matter, Roy?'

'The appointment's come through – from the hospital.'

'For the lumpectomy?'

'Yes, that.' Roy sounded uncomfortable. 'You know, we've been wondering if it's strictly necessary for your mother to go under the knife. She's not even feeling ill so how can anything be wrong?'

I raised my gaze to the ceiling and held my patience with difficulty. He was the one wondering, and I knew my mother would be easily persuaded to go along with what Roy thought best – especially if she was scared and it meant doing nothing. 'It's a minor op, not major surgery, Roy. Mum will be out the next day and the results will confirm for sure whether or not there is a problem. She must keep the appointment.'

'There's no "must" about it,' he blustered.

'Now you listen to me, Roy, and listen carefully. My mother may well feel fine now, but if the lump is cancerous she will soon become very ill and may even die if it is not dealt with quickly. I'm not trying to scare you, but I cannot emphasize too highly how important it is that Mum keeps this appointment and undergoes any further treatment if it becomes necessary. If breast cancer is caught early enough the success rate is extremely high, if not....'

There was dead silence on the end of the line and I wondered if Roy had put the phone down to go and fetch my mother. Then I heard him take a deep, shuddering breath, before he said in a voice that sounded quite unlike his usual gruff tones, 'I'll make sure she goes, but would you just have a word with her?'

'Of course,' I said. While I was waiting for my mother to come to the phone Ashlyn crept into the kitchen and held the kettle up. I nodded emphatically, 'Tea would be lovely,' then I added, 'Do you want to order a takeaway from one of the menus in the drawer? Use my mobile, it's in my bag. I might be a while.'

'Who are you talking to?' my mother's voice was sharp. 'Is Adrian there with you?'

'No, Mum, Adrian is not here with me. There's no reason he should be. We're divorced remember? I'm talking to my student lodger.'

'Student? What student? You didn't mention any student to me.'

'Oh, I'm sure I did,' I said, knowing full well that I had done no such thing, but a bit annoyed that the mother I rarely saw any more, who lived her own life without ever consulting me about the way she did it, still thought she ought to have a handle on what went on in my life. 'Ashlyn is a student at the uni. The money will come in handy and she'll be company for me.' Even as I spoke I felt cross with myself for feeling obliged to explain.

'You said you preferred your own company,' she pointed out. 'If it was company you wanted, why didn't you stay with your husband?'

'Can we not go into this again, Mum?' Furious at her censorious tone I only just refrained from demanding why she hadn't stayed with hers – my father – and had to remind myself that now was neither the time nor the place. 'Now, what's this about an appointment?'

'It's on Monday. They say they've had a cancellation and can fit me in sooner than expected.'

'Well, that's good.' I could hear Ashlyn in the other room ordering what sounded like a banquet from the local Chinese takeaway and felt my stomach growl in anticipation. It seemed a long time since I'd eaten anything.

'Oh, I don't think I'll go, you know, Franny, even though I told the lady I would. I can always ring back and cancel. It all seems a bit unnecessary. You know I don't like hospitals – I even had a home birth with you all those years ago – and an operation seems a bit drastic when I'm perfectly well. I haven't even had as much as a cold this year.'

I took a firm grip on my patience for the second time. 'This isn't a cold or flu we're talking about here, Mum, but something that could turn out to be rather more serious.'

'Well, if it is I would rather not know.' Her voice was high suddenly and scared.

'If you don't face it now, Mum, with an early diagnosis and everything on your side, you may be forced to face much worse later. If there is anything wrong, treatment now means there is every chance of a full recovery.'

'But an operation, Franny—'

'I've just explained to Roy that the surgery at this point would be quite minor and you would be in hospital no longer than twenty-four hours. Didn't you listen to the doctor before? Look at it this way, it's one day out of your life that might just save your life.'

She burst into noisy tears. 'You think I have cancer, don't you?'

'I don't think anything, love,' I kept my voice low and calm, though her hysterics were rubbing off on me and I could feel sudden fear coursing through my veins. Aggravating she might be at times but she was the only mother I had. 'That's the whole point of the tests. You're still a relatively young woman, you've just said yourself that you're healthy, now let's make sure that you stay that way.'

'What would you do if it was you?'

'I would do exactly what I'm telling you to do and you would be the first one to make sure I went for the tests. Do you want me to come to the hospital with you?'

'I think you'd better,' she said grimly, 'because Roy doesn't like hospitals any more than I do.'

I breathed a sigh of relief when I put the phone down and was grateful for the steaming cup of tea that Ashlyn put in front of me.

'Poor you,' she said, and the sympathy in her voice was enough for me to burst into tears.

She fetched tissues and paracetamol, and generally made herself useful, feeding the cat and putting plates and cutlery out ready for the Chinese that was on its way. More used to Adrian, who had fussed and flapped whenever I got upset, I did kind of appreciate her calm way of caring and the second cup of tea that immediately replaced the one I had drunk.

'You're worried aren't you?' she asked softly.

'Wouldn't you be?' I countered. 'Weren't you, when your Dad became ill?'

'He wasn't ever ill, not up to the day he died. He was absolutely fine one minute and the next he was gone. It was a heart attack at work but, thankfully, Jared was with him. It must have been traumatic for him but I'm so glad Dad didn't die alone.'

Her first words had shocked me into silence and I realized belatedly I hadn't thought to ask at any point how Mitchell Browning had died and no one had thought to tell me. 'Oh,' I said, and we fell silent each thinking our separate thoughts.

Before the silence between us could lengthen and become uncomfortable the doorbell rang, and I went to pay for the food.

'I don't know about you,' I said placing the steaming tubs and cartons out on the coffee table for us to help ourselves, 'but I'm more than ready for this.'

'Mmm,' Ashlyn popped a battered prawn into her mouth and closed her eyes in sheer enjoyment.

Conversation for a while was limited to the odd, 'Try this, and this, it's delicious,' and, 'the sauce is just fabulous, have some more.'

The TV burbled in the corner but neither of us was really watching and yet it felt quite companionable in the room and

I wondered if I could actually be getting used to having Ashlyn around. The thought was a little confusing – not to mention worrying.

'Dad would have loved this,' she said suddenly, catching me unawares. 'It's kind of sad that he can't be here to see it, right?'

Usually I thought carefully before I spoke but for once I just said what was on my mind. 'Why would he be bothered about me when he had his two point four children in Canada? In fact, why were you bothered about finding me when you already had a brother?'

'He was very bothered,' Ashlyn gave me a straight look. 'Finding you was kind of an obsession with him and I asked him once why he didn't just get on a plane and come over and find you.'

'And…?'

'He was scared, and he admitted it to me. He'd had no contact since you were a very small child – though he said that wasn't of his choosing – and you had never tried to contact him. He accepted that may well have been through choice. He didn't feel at any point in his life that he could just walk back into yours.'

'Well, he gave up that right when he walked away, didn't he? Why on earth would I try to contact him? As far as I was concerned he left and that was it, he'd simply gone away and forgotten all about me. How was I to know he and my mother were still in touch? I had no idea where he was and, as far as I knew, neither did my mother. After almost forty years of him being absent from my life the phone call from your aunt came as a complete bolt out of the blue – as did the discovery that my father had a completely new life and a new family in Canada. He even played father to other people's kids but couldn't be bothered to stay around and be a father to me.'

'Did you ever find out why?'

'No,' I said, 'did you?'

Ashlyn shook her head. 'No, as I said he never discussed it. Didn't you ever talk to your mother about any of this?' She looked puzzled – as well she might, I thought, as it was obviously what any normal person would do.

'You have to understand how difficult it was for me. She always got upset when I so much as mentioned his name, and I had this fear that if I persisted, she would leave me, too. As a child I thought my father must have left me because of something I had done wrong.'

'Oh God, that must have been so awful for you.'

'Mmm,' I muttered, and shaking my head, admitted ruefully, 'I think it's affected my behaviour and my choices right through my life – and not for the better.'

'Finding out that your mother had contact with Mitchell all these years must have come as a shock.'

'I was furious and, as you know, I immediately cut short my stay in Canada so that I could confront her – only for her to tell me the minute I saw her that she was ill.'

'You don't feel you can tackle her at the moment,' Ashlyn nodded her head. 'I would feel the same.'

'You would?'

'Well, she probably has enough to deal with right now.'

'Without me demanding answers about something she must have had her reasons for keeping to herself?'

She nodded again, 'Right.'

'Even if it means there will never be a right time to ask? Because there is a very real possibility – given the present circumstances – that time is going to run out.'

12

There, I had voiced my fear out loud. It was a fear that had remained unspoken and barely registered, except deep in my subconscious, but it had haunted me ever since my mother had stated baldly that she had cancer – even though it hadn't been confirmed.

It made me feel selfish to be thinking of myself, and my feelings at such a time, but I had been left wondering about the truth of my father's disappearance from my life for thirty-nine years. For the first time I was close to finding out what really happened because the one thing my trip to Canada had shown me was that all was not as clear cut as I had been led to believe.

I had difficulty sleeping that night with what felt like a million questions teeming through my brain. Questions that had lain dormant for years but had now surged out into the open, after my conversation with Ashlyn, and were demanding answers.

'Dad never talked about his first wife, his marriage or his reasons for leaving,' Ashlyn told me, and I had no reason to doubt her. All he had ever talked about, she had said, was finding me and trying to put things right between us – even though he had accepted that it might be far too little and far too late.

It was strange having someone to talk to after all these years, someone who knew some – if not all – of the story. As a result, some – if not all – of the resentment I'd been feeling towards her had begun to dissolve.

I still couldn't quite decide why she would want to trek across the world to insinuate herself into my life because I was quite sure that, even had I known she existed, I would not have even crossed the road to become part of hers.

I wished now I had taken up Cheryl's offer and looked more closely at the contents of the box of letters and photos in Canada. It would have been the sensible thing to do and I would probably not still be struggling to discover the truth with nothing to go on. The fact was, I had been so shocked by the apparent depth of my mother's deception that all I could feel was that I must hear the story from her own lips and not try to discover it from a bunch of old letters. That was still how I felt and I could only hope that very shortly it would become a possibility. Whatever the facts were I had to believe my mother had her reasons for concealing them from me and give her the opportunity to justify her actions.

'Have you seen Ellie?' I asked, placing a piece of toast in front of Ashlyn when she finally put in an appearance just before I was about to leave for work. 'It's not like her to miss her breakfast.'

Ashlyn bit, chewed, frowned and shook her head. 'She wasn't even on my bed last night. I thought she must have been on yours.'

'Mmm.' I wasn't overly concerned, she liked to parade around her patch, terrorizing the other cats and making a pretence at stalking birds and mice. 'Well, keep an eye out for her, would you, and feed her when she comes in? What are you up to today?'

'Thought I'd do a bit more preparation for the interview, further research into social work in the UK might be helpful,' she mused. 'Is there a library around here?'

While I was writing directions I apologized for not being able to give her a lift to the university on Monday. 'I can't trust Mum and Roy to turn up for the hospital appointment, you see. They dither between being scared to death – which is only natural, I suppose – and dismissing the whole thing as an unnecessary waste of time.'

'You'd better be there with them, right? I can manage. I don't have to be there until ten for the introductory talk and I think we get to meet current students, which will be great, you know. Then it's the individual interviews.'

I grimaced, 'The nerve wracking bit, I guess.' On my way to the door I had a sudden thought, 'What on earth are you going to wear?'

She shrugged in the universally careless way of teenagers. 'Jeans and a sweater.'

'Well, that's not going to make a very good impression, is it? Not in an English university. We'll talk about it tonight.'

Running late, I was rushing out the front door only to be hailed by Lloyd, my upstairs neighbour. As nice as he was, I found myself tutting under my breath at the delay but kept my tone friendly, and asked, 'Problem?'

'Not really sure,' he wrinkled his nose. 'I keep seeing this guy hanging around, mostly sitting in his car, but yesterday I caught him looking through your window. He said he was trying to deliver a parcel, but I wasn't convinced. The thing is, I have a feeling he has visited you before so he might just be a friend trying to catch you in.'

'Tall, fair-haired, smartly dressed?'

Lloyd nodded.

'Thought so. I do know him and I can deal with him. He's a bit of a nuisance, but nothing more. Thanks for your concern anyway.'

'You're welcome. If you want me to warn him off....'

'I'll be sure to give you a shout.'

Bloody Adrian, I fumed as I crawled through the rush hour traffic. What the hell was his game? This wasn't being caring, if anything it was a bit scary, and bordered on stalking. I made up my mind to keep an eye out for him and, if it was Adrian hanging around I was going to send him off with a well-deserved flea in his ear.

Somehow I worked through the pile of correspondence on my desk and through the thoughts piling up in my mind. My mother's health currently took precedence over everything else and I seriously hoped that Roy was going to leave it entirely to me to get her safely ensconced into a hospital bed. Having him alternately fussing and fretting on the one hand and poo-pooing the need for treatment at all on the other hand was going to have my mother in a total state and ready to run.

Then there was Ashlyn and her interview, on the same day of all things, and what I was going to do about her if she gained a place I didn't know. The sane and sensible part of me knew that I should stick to my guns and insist she live in student accommodation. After all, she wasn't my responsibility; I hadn't even known she existed just a few short weeks ago, and while we might get along all right in the short term, having a teenager in my life wasn't part of my long-term plan. I had waited too long for a life of my own to want to share it just yet.

And then there was Adrian. Bloody Adrian. Just what the hell did he think he was playing at? Exactly how many times and in how many ways did I have to tell him I didn't want him in my life before it finally sank in? Reluctantly, I thought the threat of an injunction might have to be brought into play because his behaviour was beginning to border on harassment.

I softened towards Ashlyn still further when I found a hot meal ready and waiting for me when I got home.

'It's just spaghetti bolognese,' there was an apology in her tone, 'but the sauce here in the UK is pretty good. At least, that's what the guy at the corner shop told me, so I hope it's all right.'

'Anything I don't have to cook myself is fine by me,' I insisted, twisting my fork into the pasta and then lifting it to my mouth. I nodded, 'It's lovely. Thank you.'

'I feel bad now,' she said guiltily, 'because I should have cooked for you before. I was thinking about the interview and I've decided you might be right about my appearance. I wouldn't want them to think I haven't make an effort.'

'Well,' I paused to chew another mouthful, 'we have two choices. You can either borrow something of mine, though it might swamp you, since you're shorter and slimmer – or we can go shopping.'

Her excitement was contagious and we began to plan the expedition with military precision, beginning with a list of requirements and the shops most likely to stock what Ashlyn would like.

'We should get you a decent coat,' I said, adding it to the list and realizing I was beginning to sound like the older sister in spite of myself and my determination to keep our relationship on a more casual basis. 'That little jacket you wear has no warmth to it, and the evenings can still be a bit chilly.'

'Sssh.' She held up a finger. 'Did you hear that?'

'What? I didn't hear anything. Now, about this coat.'

'It must be Ellie outside.' Ashlyn's face lit up and she ran to the French doors, sweeping the curtain back to reveal a tall figure standing there with his face pressed against the glass.

We both screamed and he disappeared, but not before I had recognized Adrian's startled face in the light from the room. Pushing Ashlyn aside I fumbled with the key and, throwing the door open, ran out after him. He was, of course, nowhere to be seen, but a few moments later there was a sharp rap at the front door.

Furiously angry I rushed to wrench it open, yelling as I did so, 'Just what the bloody hell do you think you're ...'

Adrian was standing on the doorstep but obviously not from choice because Lloyd had a firm grip on the collar of his suit and was saying, 'I heard you scream and caught him making a run for it.'

'I was just checking that you were all—'

To Adrian, I said, 'I don't want you checking that I'm all

right. I don't want you anywhere near me,' and then totally contradicting myself, I added to Lloyd, 'You'd better bring him inside.'

'Who is he? Do you know him?' Lloyd was pushing him along the hall with a firm hand in the small of his back as he spoke, and Adrian almost fell into the sitting room much to Ashlyn's very evident consternation.

'I'm her husb—'

I cut him off, correcting, 'He's my ex-husband. Something he obviously has great difficulty accepting.'

'I have the right—' Adrian began again.

'You,' I pushed a finger into his chest, 'have *no* rights over me. Our marriage is over, our relationship is over, and I won't be telling you again to stay well away from me.'

'You heard the lady,' Lloyd said sternly, 'and I shall be keeping an eye out for you in future. I've seen you skulking around.'

'Skulking around,' Adrian sounded most indignant, 'and who the hell are you anyway – the new boyfriend?'

'Adrian!' I was mortified, but Lloyd just laughed and said, 'None of your business, is it? You're the ex.'

'And who is this? Ah, the girl from the restaurant.' He looked from Ashlyn to me suspiciously, and then did a double take. You could almost see his brain working overtime as he tried to work out the connection and I thought he had it all worked out until he said, 'I get it now. I finally get it. She's your *daughter*, isn't she?'

13

Whatever the scenario I was expecting Adrian to come up with, his identifying Ashlyn as my daughter wasn't even close. I almost laughed out loud – almost but not quite.

'Don't try to deny it. You are too alike not to be related. It's quite obvious that *she*,' he pointed an accusing finger in Ashlyn's direction, 'is a dirty little secret from your past that you didn't see fit to share with me – your own husband. I suppose the guy in the restaurant is her father. Oh, yes, I can see it all now,' the torrent of sneering words poured from Adrian's mouth. 'Far from leaving our marriage for the puny excuses you used to convince me the relationship was no longer working for you, you left me to take up where you left off with your bastard's father.'

He was so pleased with his powers of deduction that he didn't even see my fist coming and it landed on his nose with a satisfying crunch that sent a jolt right up my arm. I had never so much as slapped anybody in my life and I wasn't sure who was more shocked – him or me. My knuckles throbbed but it was well worth the pain to see the look on his face.

'Bravo,' Lloyd cheered. 'If you hadn't done it I would have landed one on him myself. Did you actually used to be *married* to this jerk?'

'To my regret I have to admit that I was – and for far too long,' I said, calmly handing Adrian a box of tissues so that he could attend to his bloody nose, and saying to him at the same time, 'You're disgusting, and actually couldn't be more wrong, Adrian, but I don't expect you to believe me, and nor do I expect Ashlyn to forgive such a slanderous attack upon herself and her family. I don't expect you to believe, either, that I left you simply because I couldn't stand another day of this sort of behaviour. Now get out before I give you a cauliflower ear to go with the bloody nose.'

'When I leave here,' Adrian said, his voice muffled through a wad of bloodied tissues, 'I shall go straight to the police and have you charged with assault.'

'You can try it,' Lloyd told him flatly, 'but it won't work. There are two witnesses here to say it was a clear case of self-defence. I would take it as a lesson learned, if I were you, and stay out of your ex-wife's way in future. She's made it abundantly clear she doesn't want you around.'

Adrian turned to me and said accusingly, 'You said we could remain friends.'

It was a ridiculous thing to say given everything that had just occurred and I shook my head. 'I was wrong,' I said simply, and turned away as Lloyd took it upon himself to usher him out.

He returned only long enough to write down his mobile and home phone number and hand the piece of paper to me. 'You know where I am,' he told me, 'just a phone call away.'

Then it was just Ashlyn and me. She had listened to the whole sorry exchange in silence and I had no idea what she might have been thinking.

'I'm sorry,' I told her, 'it wasn't very nice for you to be involved in that.'

She looked pale and shaken and sank into the nearest chair. 'Jesus,' she said, 'Whatever made you get involved with a guy like that?'

I was suddenly angry at what sounded a tad too judgemental for my taste and felt an almost violent need to defend my choice of a husband. 'I was young when I met him, and having grown up feeling unloved and abandoned I found it hard to trust anyone. In those circumstances it's easy to confuse control for caring.'

Ashlyn sprang to her feet, practically bristling with fury. 'I hope you're not saying it's Dad's fault you married an arsehole,' she fumed. 'You aren't the only kid to grow up without a father and he must have had his reasons for leaving when he did.'

'What reason can justify leaving a little child bewildered and grieving? Tell me that? If he had his reasons he should have stayed around long enough to bloody well tell me what they were. It was the very least he could do before he buggered off and created another family thousands of miles from the one he left behind. How do you think it made me feel discovering *that* on the day of his funeral?'

'You think it was hard for you? How the hell do you think I felt growing up in the shadow of this other daughter away across the sea? The perfect child who could do no wrong and was spoken of in hushed tones and longed for every single day. All the children in the world – subsequently fostered or born to him – couldn't make up to Dad for not having you in his life and yet he never stopped trying to salve his conscience for leaving you, even if it was with taking in other people's kids. Oh, I knew he loved me in his own way, but I never stopped feeling like a substitute for the precious child he left behind in England, right up until the day he died.'

I was shocked into silence and just stared at her for a long, long moment, until I managed, in little more than a whisper, 'I never knew you felt like that.'

'How could you when you obviously never gave a thought to anyone's feelings but your own?' Ashlyn said bitterly and, shrugging me away when I reached out to touch her, she added, 'Leave me alone. I made a big mistake coming here, but that's easily rectified and I will be leaving for Canada as soon as I can get a flight.'

'But you have an interview – we were going shopping.' Even as I protested I was wondering why I was arguing. I should have been delighted that she was going. After all, it was what I had wanted ever since she'd arrived, wasn't it? I just knew in my heart and despite my misgivings that I didn't want her to leave – not like this – not with yet more blame and bitterness thrown into a mix that went back years, apparently filled with misunderstandings.

Ashlyn shrugged her slim shoulders. 'Who cares?' she said, 'I know when I'm not wanted. This whole thing was a huge mistake.'

'But not our mistake, Ashlyn, you can't blame me for being born, any more than I can blame you. I admit I resented you as soon as I knew of your existence, and envied you for all those years with our father that I didn't have. It's only now we're having this discussion that I can see how foolish I was being. We're both victims of a past that was totally out of our control.' I managed a smile, 'I know I'm not much of a sister, but I'm actually the only one you've got and, given the chance, I'm sure I can do better than I have so far.'

There was a stubborn look on her face, but gradually a reluctant smile replaced it and she muttered, 'You haven't done so badly, you know.'

'Really?'

She laughed then. 'I don't think there are too many people who would have taken me in after I'd arrived uninvited on their doorstep. Probably a good thing we got that stuff out into the open just now, too, instead of harbouring old grudges.'

'Funny how we were resentful of each other for similar reasons; I would never have dreamed you felt that way, too, but now I know I can understand. Did he really talk about me?' I asked and could hear the wistful note in my voice.

'All the time, from when I was a little girl, but nothing about why he was there in Canada and you were here in the UK, or about why he never saw you or spoke to you. You'll have to find out the truth, right?'

I nodded, 'Just as soon as the time is right. It's something we both need to know, I feel.'

'I think we do.'

'So, you'll stay then.'

'If you'll have me.'

'It will be my pleasure – I think,' I said, and we both

laughed, and I, at least, could actually feel the atmosphere lighten.

We ate breakfast together the following morning in a glum mood despite our improved relationship. The cause was our shared concern over Ellie, because there was still no sign of her. There was a real reason to worry, since she had never gone missing for more than a few hours before; she was too fond of her food for that.

'I could call round the neighbours,' Ashlyn offered, 'and ask them to check their sheds and garages in case she's been locked in.'

'Oh, that's a great idea,' I said warmly, 'I'm sure she can't be far away.'

'Unless someone has taken her.' Ashlyn was only saying pretty much what we were both thinking, but I stared at her in consternation.

'Who would do such a thing?' I wondered out loud, and our gazes met and mirrored the same worrying thought. 'He wouldn't dare,' I said flatly.

'Are you sure?' she queried softly and I knew that I wasn't.

'If I find out he has,' I fumed, 'he will get more than a bloodied nose for his efforts. Let's give him the benefit of the doubt for now and presume he hasn't. You pop round the neighbours quickly while I wash up and we can get going. Ellie will probably be here waiting when we get back.'

Shopping with a teenager was a whole different experience than with my mother and quite a lot of fun, I found. Ashlyn insisted I also try on clothes and often they were garments that I would have considered far too young for me. It was surprising how good I often felt and looked in them.

'God, you're only in your forties,' Ashlyn reminded me, 'and you have a great figure but, though you dress nicely, you don't really do yourself any favours, do you?'

'I'm a bit old for crop tops and skinny jeans,' I kept my tone light, but the criticism stung a bit. 'At my age I have to be careful not to come over as mutton dressed as lamb.'

'Perhaps not cropped tops, then,' she allowed kindly, 'but those skinny jeans you tried would look great tucked into a pair of boots. You have amazing legs and could show them off in those and the knee-length straight skirts everyone seems to be wearing at the moment.'

Looking around a store that was getting quite crowded I could see with my own eyes that she was right. I relented with an air of what-the-hell that was quite foreign to me. I rarely went shopping – and the session with my mother had been the first in years. Usually I was alone with no one but an assistant eager to make a sale to voice an opinion on what suited and what didn't. When shopping online – which was my usual method – I tended to go for companies catering for my age range and chose safe options, which I now realized might have been labelled boring.

Ashlyn and I did come close, however, to disagreeing over what might or might not be suitable for an interview.

'Buying a suit I will never wear again is a waste of money,' she said flatly. 'No one will expect young girls applying for a university course to get dressed up.'

'I think you're wrong about that, and first impressions count for quite a lot. After all, you are applying for a course that will lead to a career in social work. Why would you want to look as if you hadn't made any effort when a professional demeanour might just make all the difference? I know it's only clothes, but appearances are important. Who would you offer a place to, someone in jeans or someone in a suit?'

'The one who performed well at interview,' Ashlyn insisted stubbornly, 'whatever they were wearing.'

'OK,' I allowed, 'but if it came to a choice between two people, wouldn't you go for the one that offered the whole package and looked and behaved professionally?'

'It's a waste of money.'

I recognized the jut to the jaw and knew I was going to have my work cut out if I wanted to get my own way.

'Just humour me and try on one or two,' I pleaded, 'and if you look like a dork I will concede defeat.'

'A dork is an idiot, right?'

I nodded, and, thrusting a handful of suits on the hangers at her, I pushed her towards the changing rooms and reminded her, 'I want to see how they look, so don't forget to come out and show me. Give me your handbag – purse – and I'll take care of it while you're in there.'

Ashlyn looked amazing in every one of the suits, black or navy, skirt or trousers. She looked grown up and yet still very young and the dark colours set off her long blonde hair and youthful complexion.

As we stood side-by-side looking in the mirror at her reflection in a particularly well cut trouser suit, an elderly couple nearby smiled at us and the lady said, 'You must be so proud of your daughter. She's very beautiful.'

'She's my sister,' I said, 'and I am very proud of her.'

Ashlyn beamed up at me and, as I smiled back I felt sure I could feel the beginning of an unshakeable bond growing between us.

'How can I refuse to wear the suit after that?'

I laughed. 'How indeed? I would like to buy it for you, with any accessories you choose to make up the outfit.'

'There's no need, I have money.'

'Which will soon dwindle away when you are a student,' I reminded her. 'Anyway, I'm your big sister and I'm allowed to treat you – and I have several years to make up for, remember. I won't be offended if you don't wear any of it again after the interview, I promise.'

With the glossy carrier dangling from Ashlyn's fingers we stepped back out onto the street and I was all set to go back to the car.

'Oh, no,' Ashlyn stopped me with a firm hand on my arm, 'now that I've allowed you to dress me, you must let me return the favour,' she insisted, dragging me back to Zara and holding out the skinny jeans I had already tried on.

Once I was wearing them teamed with a long sweater in grey and matching boots, I found my previous objections just melted away because I did look like a younger and funkier version of me – and I liked it.

It didn't take much to persuade me to make a day of it and with a lunch of paninis and afternoon tea slotted into the day, it was getting late by the time we returned home. I had trouble parking the car, which was annoying, but not unusual, given that I lived in a built-up area with very little off-road parking. We shared out the assorted carrier bags and were promising ourselves a nice hot cup of tea as we turned into the gate with Ashlyn slightly in front of me.

I heard her give a horrified gasp and watched the carrier bags slip from her fingers as she made a dash forward. Hurrying after her, I spotted the lifeless body of Ellie on the front step at the same moment as Ashlyn burst into tears.

'She's dead!' she cried. 'Ellie's dead – and he's killed her.'

14

I stared down at the little cat, at the pretty fur all matted now and the closed eyes. There was a trickle of blood coming from her nose and mouth and that convinced me that she was quite dead. I felt a great well of grief building inside of me as I reached out to smooth Ellie's sweet head knowing that this time no rumbling purr would greet me.

'What's the matter? What's happened?' Lloyd must have come through the gate behind us because suddenly he was pushing us both aside, kneeling beside Ellie and touching her with gentle fingers. 'Where's your car?' he asked urgently.

'My car?' I looked at him stupidly.

'To get her to a vet,' he said, explaining, 'there's a slight pulse.' He was already removing his jacket, lifting the cat gently and lovingly wrapping her in its folds.

I ran, leaving the bags I'd been carrying scattered all over the path. Back to the car in seconds, my hand shook as I tried to insert the key into the ignition and then with the engine roaring I sped to where they stood waiting at the kerbside and screeched to a halt. Lloyd climbed into the front holding Ellie like a baby and Ashlyn threw all the bags in the back and fell in after them.

As we pulled away I saw Adrian standing at the corner of the road. He watched us pass with a strange expression on his face, and I knew, I just knew without any shadow of a doubt that he was responsible for whatever had happened to my cat. I experienced a fury such as I had never known and tightened my hands on the steering wheel lest the temptation to run him over proved too much to resist. I made myself a promise that he wouldn't get away with this, but acknowledged that he wasn't important right at that moment.

I had barely brought the car to a halt in front of the large building that housed the veterinary practice I used before Lloyd was out of the car and racing towards the door. He was inside before either of us was out of the car and we followed, the dread we were feeling etched clearly on each of our faces. I think we had already prepared ourselves for the worst before we had opened the door to follow Lloyd inside.

The reception area was unmanned and, just a handful of customers waited with their animal patients.

'They went through there.' A man with an overweight Rottweiler panting at his side indicated the rear of the premises with a vague wave of his arm. 'Your cat, is it? It looked in a bad way,' he added helpfully.

Ignoring him, I successfully fought the urge to rush after them and took hold of Ashlyn's arm in case she had a similar idea. We stood by the receptionist's desk and looked at each other helplessly. After what seemed an age a veterinarian nurse came through, followed by Lloyd. They were empty handed and they both looked grim.

'Is she...? Is she...?' I couldn't say the word and Ashlyn

promptly burst into tears all over again.

'She's alive,' the nurse said gently and I heard Lloyd mutter, 'Just,' under his breath.

The nurse went on to talk about drips and shock, about stabilizing and seeing how she went. The advice was that we should go home and wait. They would ring us with any news. I was too afraid to ask her to speculate on what form she thought that 'news' might take.

'I'll drive back, shall I?' Lloyd took the keys from my nerveless fingers, and I was glad to give the responsibility to him. Especially since I couldn't recall a single minute of the journey we had just made to the vet's, even though I was aware that I was the one driving.

When we reached home Lloyd was the one to gather up the bags, to usher us inside, to turn up the heating and make hot sweet tea, while we just huddled together and tried to still the chattering of our teeth.

'At least she has a fighting chance,' Lloyd did his best to assure us.

'No thanks to me,' I said bitterly, 'I thought she was already—'

'We both did,' Ashlyn put in. 'What do you think happened, Lloyd?'

He shook his head and shrugged. 'I honestly don't know – a car, poison, she might just be ill.'

'Whatever happened, it has something to do with *him*.' I felt I had to say it out loud or I might have burst from the effort of keeping my suspicion in.

'No,' Ashlyn whispered, 'he wouldn't really do something like that – would he?'

'Him?' Lloyd stared at me and then ventured a guess. 'The ex?'

I nodded grimly. 'Didn't you see him when we pulled away earlier – watching us?'

They both shook their heads.

'I think you should phone the police,' Ashlyn said emphatically.

'And tell them what?' I asked. 'We don't have a single scrap of proof and he's a well respected man without so much as the hint of a stain on his character. No one would believe us.'

Ashlyn looked at Lloyd and he lifted his shoulders helplessly. 'Fran is right,' he said. 'Not much the police can do without some sort of concrete evidence.' He turned to me. 'You might want to keep a diary of everything he's done so far, though, even if you only suspect it, and anything he might get up to from now on. Make a note of witnesses – like the time the three of us were here. I think we all know he's not going to give up and go away anytime soon. I will say again, and I hope you know I mean it, you know where I am if you need me, anytime, day or night.'

'It's really very nice of you, Lloyd, but you barely know me. We'd scarcely exchanged a word until recently. I wouldn't like you to feel that you have to get involved in my clashes with Adrian.' I was actually thinking it would hardly be surprising if he had made a point of running away as fast as his legs could carry him. Who needed these complications in their lives, after all? 'Thank you so much for what you did for Ellie today, though. If she survives it will only be because of your prompt actions.'

'I'm glad I could help,' he said and his smile was kind,

sympathetic, and I thought what a very nice man he was. 'I suppose I should be grateful to the guy – much as it grieves me to say it – because I've been looking for an excuse to do more than pass the time of day with you ever since you moved in.'

'Really?' I was ridiculously pleased and flattered.

'Really,' he said smiling, and there was a look in his eyes that made my toes curl deliciously.

He was on his way to the door when the phone rang and I think we all jumped; certainly Ashlyn and I stared at the instrument in absolute terror and neither of us made a move to answer the call.

'Would you like me to get it?' Lloyd offered and we nodded mutely and then stood hugging each other while he did just that. He was nodding, even though the person on the other end of the line wouldn't be able to see that. 'I see,' he said seriously, 'yes, I see. Mmm, I understand.' Replacing the receiver he turned to us and I know that I, at least, stopped breathing.

'Ellie is still with us and they believe they have her condition stabilized, though it sounds as if it was touch and go for a while there. The shock, you know, that's the biggest killer of all. They think she may have been hit by a car, but don't yet know the extent of her injuries and are loath to pull her about at the moment. Tomorrow they will X-ray Ellie and check for any internal damage. They will ring if there's any change, but will be able to let us know more in the morning. Are you all right?'

I nodded, tears streaming down my cheeks. 'Thank you, Lloyd, thank you so much.'

He patted my shoulder awkwardly and advised, 'You know where I am,' and then he was gone.

'Nice guy,' Ashlyn said with great feeling.

'He is,' I agreed, 'and yet I never spoke to him before you came. I should make more effort with the neighbours, talk to people the way you do, but I've always found it hard to make friends.'

'I'm sure they would all be looking out for you if they knew you were having problems with, you know, *him*. Do you really think he might have taken the cat?'

'Well, I did,' I started collecting the bags of shopping that were strewn around, 'but even he couldn't have arranged for her to be run over – could he?'

Ashlyn pulled a face. 'I wouldn't put anything past that guy, but … probably not. Where has she been, though, for the past few days? You said yourself she never goes off for more than a few hours.'

'If—' I stopped myself right there and went on, '*When* Ellie comes home, she is not going outside again until I am absolutely certain that she will be safe. I had to do it when I first took her in and I will just have to do it again.'

'Won't she hate that?'

We carried on talking from our respective bedrooms as we unpacked and hung away our purchases. All the pleasure we had enjoyed in the buying of the garments had long since faded away and I felt as if I never wanted to look at the clothes again. If only we'd been at home when Ellie had turned up on the step, action could have been taken sooner, and we might even have caught the culprit.

However, when morning came it brought good news from

the vet. Ellie was making a surprisingly swift recovery from injuries that were nowhere near as serious as was first thought.

Grinning from ear to ear, I practically bounced into Ashlyn's room, threw back the curtains with a flourish to let the sunshine in, and encouraged, 'Come on, it's a beautiful day and *we* are going out for breakfast.'

'We are?' First, the top of her tousled blonde head appeared from beneath the covers, followed by a sleepy face and blue eyes blinking against the sudden bright light. 'What about...?'

'Ellie should be home by tonight. It appears she was shocked, very bruised and dehydrated, but there are no internal injuries. She should make a full recovery and we can go and see her as soon as we're ready.'

The rest of Ashlyn made a sudden appearance as she threw back the quilt and shot across the room to wrap me in a bear hug. I had absolutely no reservations about hugging her back and then we stood for a moment grinning happily at each other.

'Where are we going?'

'Once we've visited Ellie, you, my dear sister, are going to try a traditional full English breakfast.'

'Oh, Dad cooked those for us kids all the time.' Ashlyn spoke without thinking and I could tell from her face that she wished she hadn't.

I ignored the pang I felt at all those breakfasts I had missed out on and said lightly, 'A full English breakfast, cooked in England, cannot be compared to anything remotely resembling the meal that was cooked elsewhere. The ingredients, not to mention cooking methods, will be entirely different and so, therefore, will the resulting flavour.'

Already on her way to the bathroom she stopped suddenly. 'Wear your new jeans,' she pleaded, adding quickly, 'but don't expect me to wear my new suit.'

'I wouldn't dream of it,' I assured her, 'because you'd probably drop egg yolk down the front just to spite me.'

'As if I'd do such a thing. No, I now bow to your superior knowledge of the interview process in the UK and accept that smart dress is the accepted thing, first impressions and all that. I'll run up and ask Lloyd if he wants to join us, shall I?'

She was gone before I could think of a reason to stop her, and I think we were both disappointed when he proved to be out.

At the vet's we were shown Ellie reclining in a cage on a fleecy blanket; her foreleg had been shaved where the drip had gone in and she had, apparently spent some time in an oxygen tent. I was allowed to smooth her pretty head and was rewarded by the sound of the familiar rumbling purr that brought tears of relief to my eyes.

We drove to a greasy spoon transport café that was open seven days a week, and was obviously popular judging by the number of cars and lorries parked outside.

Ashlyn decided to try everything that was on the breakfast menu piled onto one enormous plate, although it was obvious that some things she had never even heard of. I think even the long distance lorry drivers around us were impressed when she managed to clear the lot – apart from the black pudding. Everyone agreed it was a delicacy to some but an acquired taste for others and gave her a standing ovation when she swallowed the last piece of toast.

'I don't think skinny jeans are the best mode of dress for this type of eating out,' I said ruefully, pulling at a waistband that seemed to have shrunk by several inches in the hour or so we'd been inside the café. 'And how you haven't burst wide open after that little lot, I will never know.'

The rest of the day was spent at home lazily reading the Sunday papers in my case and watching American sitcoms in Ashlyn's. A litter tray was prepared ready for Ellie's eagerly awaited homecoming, together with the little bed she'd never used – preferring my bed or the most comfy chair – just in case it was more to her taste now that she was fragile.

'You really ought to think about preparation for the interview,' I told Ashlyn, in an effort to take my mind away from a telephone that remained stubbornly silent as the time crept towards early evening with no word from the vet.

As she opened her mouth to reply it did ring and we both visibly jumped. My hand was shaking as I reached out and, lifting the phone, said, 'Francesca Dudly, can I help you?' just as if I were at work.

'Just phoning to see how you are.'

I couldn't believe it was Adrian on the phone, and acting as if the past few days hadn't even happened. I was torn between either slamming the phone down on him or screaming expletives into his ear.

'What the hell do you think you are doing,' I hissed in the end, keeping a firm grip on my temper, 'ringing me as if nothing has happened? What will it take to make you *leave.*

Me. Alone?' Despite a very concerted effort on my part I could hear my voice rising and my tone sharpening.

'I just want to help. It's all I've ever wanted.' He sounded as if butter wouldn't melt, but I knew otherwise.

'By stalking me? Yes, stalking,' I insisted, when he tried to interrupt, 'so that I can't turn around without tripping over you. By stealing my cat and practically killing her.'

'No,' he sounded horrified, and then I was horrified when he continued, 'that wasn't meant to happen.'

'What?' I demanded in a voice that was deceptively calm. 'What wasn't meant to happen, Adrian?'

'Well,' he stalled for a minute and then it all came tumbling out. 'I just borrowed her for a few days. To worry you a little bit, so that you would be grateful when I found her for you – but then she suddenly clawed me as I carried her down your road. I dropped her, she ran, and there was a car coming. If she hadn't struggled—'

'So it's Ellie's own fault she ended up on my doorstep as good as dead? Is that what you're saying?' I couldn't believe what I was hearing.

'I didn't mean for that to happen.'

'You never mean for any of the things you do to happen, do you, Adrian? You never meant to make my life a misery with your controlling ways, never meant to cause the jealous scenes that embarrassed us both throughout our marriage, never meant to isolate me from my friends, but it never stopped you, did it? This time your thoughtless behaviour put a cat's life in danger, next time it might be a person. In future I would think twice about the possible consequences before you act.'

'I will. I promise you I will. I can change,' Adrian's voice took on a desperate note but I was a long way past feeling sorry for him. 'If you give me the chance I can make it all up to you.'

'Nothing you do in the future, Adrian, can ever make up for everything you have done in the past. Try taking responsibility for your own actions because simply saying, "I didn't mean it", is no defence and one day that attitude is going to get you into serious trouble. However, that is not my problem, *you* are not my problem. You've had all the chances I'm prepared to give.'

'You don't mean it.'

'Yes,' I said firmly, 'I do. Unlike you I don't say or do things that I don't mean.'

There was silence on the other end of the phone and, certain that Adrian had finally got the message, I carefully replaced the receiver.

15

In the end I was advised that it was probably best Ellie didn't come home that night, though the vet was at great pains to assure me that she was recovering nicely, but they would just prefer her to stay on the drip for a while longer. I explained about my mother and the hospital appointment the following day and so it was arranged that I would collect her at the end of the day.

'There's always someone on duty,' they assured me.

'Probably for the best, right?' Ashlyn had pointed out, 'since there'll be nobody at home tomorrow to keep an eye on her for most of the day, but I'll be home all day the day after.'

In the cold light of the following morning, I told Ashlyn, 'I don't think Adrian will dare show his face round here again, and I doubt Ellie will be allowed outside for a while anyway, but just as a precaution I shall be keeping her safely indoors for the foreseeable future. Better safe than sorry.'

'I think you're absolutely right,' she agreed nodding. 'What sort of man is he, anyway, that he can't even be trusted with a cat? There's something odd about him and you did well to get out of that relationship in one piece.'

I couldn't help laughing and said, 'He's not *dangerous*, Ashlyn, just stupid sometimes. He acts without thinking.'

'*Exactly*,' she said with emphasis.

'Anyway, what about you?' I watched her chew on another piece of toast – her third full-sized slice, all of them spread thickly with butter – and was amazed that any last minute nerves about attending the interview didn't seem to have affected her appetite in any way. At her age and in her position I would have chewed my nails to the quick by now, and given the toast a wide berth. 'Are sure you're all right going to the interview on your own?'

Ashlyn smiled, 'Why? Were you thinking of coming along to hold my hand, because they wouldn't let you stay anyway, you know? I'm sure dragging parents along to an interview – never mind a sibling – would give the impression you probably wouldn't be able to cope with even the simplest things in life by yourself.'

'I'd have liked to be able to have dropped you off at the door at least. I thought Jared was going to try and make it, but it's a very long way to come and we both know how busy he is.'

I'd been almost certain he would show up and was surprised by how disappointed I was that he hadn't. Of course, I quickly assured myself, my disappointment was only for Ashlyn and it wouldn't bother me if I never saw him again. After all, he was no relation to me.

'I think he knows well enough that if I can find my way halfway around the world I can certainly manage to get on the right bus for a ten minute ride.'

I knew she was right, but I still felt very torn. It was such bad luck that my mother's hospital appointment and Ashlyn's interview were on the same day. I reminded myself that at least Ashlyn could be trusted to keep her appointment, whereas it was down to me to make sure my mother kept hers.

Wishing Ashlyn good luck, I set off to collect my mother, allowing ample time for any last minute cajoling I might have to do and for the persistent and repeated tours of the car park we would probably face when we arrived at the hospital. Car spaces at Brankstone Hospital were as limited as they were at every other hospital it had ever been my misfortune to visit. The prices, charged by the hour, should surely provide enough to build a multi-storey car park on every site, I mused sourly as I waited for a red traffic light to change, but that never seemed to be the case. I just hoped my mother didn't keep me waiting or worse, refuse point blank to keep the appointment at all, or we'd never get there and parked in time.

She must have been watching out for me because the front door opened before I even had time to put on the handbrake, and I kept the engine running. She was wearing one of the new outfits we had bought, I noticed with pleasure, and her hair still looked very pretty, though her face was a bit paler than usual.

'You look good,' I commented as she climbed in beside me. 'Where's Roy?' I looked back at the house expectantly, 'I did tell him I wanted to get an early start.'

'He's not coming.'

'Not coming?'

'That's what I said.'

'Something else on?' I put the car in gear, indicated, pulled out into a steady stream of traffic and then glanced at her set face. 'What happened? Did you two have a fight?'

'He didn't want me to come. Started saying again that all this surely wasn't necessary and why was I even bothering.'

I could feel myself getting hot and angry on her account, but then I told myself what he thought wasn't important at that moment – though his selfishness and lack of support must be upsetting for my mother, he was her husband, after all. I thought he was probably very scared, but that didn't excuse him. This definitely wasn't the time to be thinking of himself or for burying his head in the sand.

'Well, I'm glad you didn't listen to him, Mum. He's a man, what does he know?'

'He was very rude about you.'

I nodded. I could just imagine. 'His opinion of me doesn't matter. His opinion of what we're doing today doesn't matter, either. We're going to the hospital to get the opinion of an expert – that's what matters.'

My mother smiled. 'You sound just like your ...' she stopped suddenly and then hurried on, 'like an expert yourself.'

She had been going to say I sounded just like my father, I just knew it and I wondered where on earth that had come from. She had never so much as mentioned his name from the day he left all those years ago, and I was quite sure she would sooner have bitten her tongue off than to compare me to a man she clearly despised. It sounded to me as if her guard was finally slipping. I hoped so – I really hoped so.

I thought the gods must be smiling down on us – or perhaps it was even my father finally taking care of us in the role of a parking angel – because we drove into the car park and straight into a parking place as someone pulled out right in front of us.

'Wow,' I said, as I came round to open the door for her, 'that was a bit of luck.'

'We are rather early so there was plenty of time,' she pointed out, and then pushing my proffered hand away, she said touchily, 'I can manage. I'm not sick – yet.'

'I'll take your bag then. Do you have everything you need in here?'

'Everything from the list they gave me.'

I was about to suggest getting a cup of tea from the little café run by the WRVS, but remembered just in time that Mum wasn't allowed to eat or drink.

'Anything you want from the shop? A newspaper, magazines?'

'I wouldn't be able to concentrate. You're not going to leave me on my own, are you?' she suddenly sounded terrified.

'Not for a minute, I'll be there until you go in to theatre and the first person you see when you open your eyes.' I thought my voice sounded a little bit too hearty, but she didn't seem to notice.

Following the signs for the day surgery wards, I slowed my pace to match hers and felt quite touched when she tucked her hand into the crook of my arm. I knew the decision to support my mother rather than Ashlyn today had been the right one but I was still very cross with Roy for letting her down. I felt sure I could feel her shaking when we stepped into the lift and knew I'd have been as nervous myself in the same situation.

Her name was ticked off a list at the reception desk and a nurse came to show us the way to a four-bedded bay. Two of the beds already had curtains pulled around them; we were shown to the third and before long someone else was taking possession of the fourth and final bed.

Predictably, my mother didn't want my help getting into the hospital gown – not even with the ties at the back. I wasn't sure how she was going to manage but just accepted that she would and concentrated on the view from the window, which was, inevitably, a bird's eye view of the car park.

From so high up the vehicles below looked like Dinky toys and there was one that looked suspiciously like Roy's navy blue Volvo going round and round. However, since I wasn't anticipating that he would have a change of heart, I certainly wasn't going to mention it and build my mother's hopes up.

When I turned, she was sitting up in the high bed and looking absolutely terrified. It was a look that was mirrored on the face of each of the other three patients, despite their differing appearances.

The lady opposite looked as if she might be in her seventies or even her eighties, with hair that was white and tightly curled. A man who must have been her husband hovered over her, tucking in the sheet and making sure her pillows were plumped up. The way he looked at her and patted her hand brought a huge lump to my throat. He obviously loved her very much and didn't care who knew it.

Diagonally across was a girl who looked barely out of her teens and with her was a woman who was probably her mother, since they looked incredibly alike despite the obvious difference in their ages. The mother actually looked more concerned than the girl, who was lounging back against the pillows and flicking through what looked like one of those glossy celebrity magazines. She gave the appearance of not having a care in the world.

The final patient was a woman of around my own age and both she and the man with her looked as if they would sooner have been anywhere else in the world than in that hospital ward. They weren't speaking and barely even glanced at each other.

There was a flurry of activity as name bracelets were checked and looped around the correct wrist. I decided to make myself scarce when paperwork was produced and further checks appeared to be imminent.

'I'll just be outside,' I said, making my way to the door, which flew open just as I reached it and I was nearly bowled over by Roy's not insubstantial figure rushing in. He was sweating profusely and totally out of breath. I turned to my mother with a smile and said, 'Look who's here.'

'Mmmm-mmmmm-mmmmm,' she said around a thermometer, but her eyes lit up and she beamed as best she could.

'I couldn't let her go through that on her own,' he said gruffly, quite some time later when we had seen her off to theatre with a great show of cheery confidence which disappeared the minute she was out of sight. Realizing what he'd said, he hastily corrected, 'Well, I knew you were with her, but I am her husband.'

I refrained from telling him it was about time he began

acting like one, especially when he added, 'I was scared. Well, terrified if I'm honest, and I did have trouble believing there might be something wrong when Joan always looks so well.'

'You're here now and that's the main thing.'

The day passed in a blur. We fretted and worried until my mother was safe – if a little sleepy – and back in her bed, and then we all fretted and worried about what the verdict might be.

It wasn't until I finally drove away from the hospital that I remembered I had to go and collect Ellie from the vet and that I hadn't given so much as a thought to Ashlyn or her interview. Belatedly, I hoped it had gone well for her. I would cross the bridge of her staying as a student in this country if it came to that.

I tried to ring her as soon as I reached the vet's – I tried her mobile and the house phone – but she wasn't answering either. I left a similar message on each, saying I hoped the day had gone well and looked forward to hearing all about it.

Ellie looked surprisingly very much like her old self after her ordeal. I was advised to keep her indoors for two weeks but had already decided to keep her in for longer anyway. I settled a bill that made my eyes water quite a bit and determined to make sure that Adrian reimbursed me for every penny.

I let myself into the flat, calling Ashlyn's name even though I could already tell she wasn't at home. The silence was deafening. It was odd how much I missed her presence and the way she brought the place to life, even though she had been living with me for only a relatively short time.

I locked the catflap before opening Ellie's catcarrier, and quickly double-checked that the door and all the windows were closed. She seemed to be suffering no ill effects, and after eating a whole sachet of food she scorned the cat bed to stretch out on the couch.

I thought I might find a note from Ashlyn saying she had popped out, but there was nothing and a quick look in her bedroom was enough to convince me that she hadn't been home since the interview. The only message on the answer-phone was from me and she still wasn't answering her mobile. I felt a twinge of disquiet and wondered where on earth she could be. She hadn't really been out on her own since she arrived, and apart from the neighbours she had made no friends that I knew of.

I rang her mobile again. 'Ashlyn, where are you? Please ring me. If you need a lift I can come and get you, but ring me anyway.'

I found myself pacing the flat, alternating between getting angry and worrying about what might have happened to her. I couldn't believe she could be so selfish, going off like that when she knew I had enough to think about with my mother. Was she punishing me for not making her my priority? Surely not, I found myself shaking my head, because even as young as she was she could surely accept a serious health scare came before an interview.

I should have thought to phone her after the interview, of course, but with both Roy and my mother practically in pieces I'd had my work cut out calming them down and trying to deal with unanswerable questions like, 'What if it's spread?'

The street outside was growing dark and I watched Ellie make her way to the cat flap and butt it gently with her head. When it didn't open, she pushed with more force and looking back at me, she meowed and then went back to trying.

'Sorry, sweetie,' I said, carrying her to the litter tray, 'you're confined to quarters for the time being. Vet's orders – and just in case Adrian gets any other bright ideas concerning you. He probably didn't mean to hurt you, but he almost managed to get you killed and we're taking no chances. Now where is that girl?'

In that heart-stopping moment I put two and two together and came up with a big fat four. The ice cold of a very real fear trickled into my veins. I tried hard to dismiss the very idea from my mind. It was ridiculous and I was sure Adrian wouldn't do such a thing. Kidnapping a cat was one thing, but a teenage girl....

And then I remembered he'd convinced himself that Ashlyn was my daughter and I knew that he would.

16

I found myself pacing up and down, completely beside myself, and more convinced by the minute that Adrian had taken Ashlyn, just as he had taken Ellie. He must have totally lost the plot to do something so hare-brained, but it was what he was going to do with her now that he had her that caused me the most concern. As certain as I was that he would not intentionally harm the girl, recalling what had happened to Ellie I felt very scared for Ashlyn. What if she tried to escape and came to grief as the cat had done?

I should phone the police. My hand had reached for the phone, was touching it, and then I hesitated, forcing myself to face the facts. Ashlyn was eighteen years old, an adult and free to come and go as she chose. In real terms she had been missing no time at all and it was scarcely dark yet. I had no proof at all that Adrian had snatched her and it sounded too far-fetched to be true, even to my suspicious mind. It would be my word against his that he had taken Ellie and caused her harm – however unintentionally – because no one else had heard his admission of guilt.

All I had to go on was a gut instinct, a cold hard feeling of dread in my stomach that all was not right and the undisputed fact that Ashlyn had not returned home after the social work interview and was still not answering her phone several hours later.

Trying to be sensible, I paused to wonder if it was just me she wasn't talking to. What about her family? Jared and her mother, might she have phoned them to talk about how she had got on, assuming that I didn't care because I had put my own mother first?

I found the number for the family home in Canada, tapping it in quickly before I could change my mind. Then I didn't know what to say when Cheryl answered, sounding bright and bubbly, and not the least bit concerned – though it soon became clear that she hadn't heard from Ashlyn either.

'I was just saying to Julie, you know, that I was expecting to hear from Ashlyn the minute the interview was over. Is she there? How did she get on?'

For a moment I was lost for words, realizing there was no way I could say I didn't know and start a major panic far away in British Columbia when Ashlyn could turn up at any minute.

'She's popped out,' I lied, trying to match her light tone and crossing my fingers, I added, 'it went really well, but she'll be telling you all about it herself. Um, is Jared there?'

'He was called over to Vancouver to sort something out, though it had been his intention to pay a flying visit to the UK. You can get him on his cell phone.'

The rest of the call was a blur to me but I must have made all the right responses in all the right places. As I hung up,

I thought with dread about making a return call to tell Cheryl her daughter was missing, had been for some time and that I had been lying through my teeth throughout the earlier call.

I tried Ashlyn's phone again and was unsurprised when it went to voicemail. 'Call me,' was all I said. I tried Jared's and the same thing happened, though I left no message. When I finally tried Adrian's, the home phone remained unanswered and his mobile was switched off. That was all it took to convince me that he had taken Ashlyn, because Adrian just never turned his phone off. I had only punched in the first nine for an emergency call when the doorbell rang, loud and long.

She was back. Ashlyn was home. Oh, thank God, thank God. On legs that felt as limp as boiled spaghetti, I staggered to the door, but I knew before I opened it that it wasn't Ashlyn because the shadow through the glass was too tall, too bulky. It had to be....

'Just what the bloody hell do you think you're playing at, you bloody mad man?' I fumed, and wasn't sure who was more startled, the man I found standing on the step or me.

'Well,' Jared drawled, 'I've been called some things in my time.'

Suddenly realizing that Ellie was squeezing between my legs and about to escape, I slammed the door in Jared's face. Only when she was shut in my bedroom with the litter tray did I go back and open the door. He didn't appear to have moved an inch.

'Well, I realize we didn't hit it off in the beginning, but I hadn't realized things were that bad between us. I've obviously done something to seriously upset you,' he said, 'but I can't think for the life of me what that might be.'

I pushed past him, looked up and down the street and then went back inside pulling him with me.

'Did you see anyone hanging around out there?' I demanded, and when he didn't answer immediately, said sharply, 'Think, this is important.'

He shrugged, and looked at me as if I were the mad one, 'No one obvious, but it is quite a busy street and people are still coming home from work I would imagine.' His dark eyes narrowed suddenly. 'This isn't about that ex-husband of yours, is it? Jeez, I knew he was trouble the minute I clapped eyes on him. What's he done now?' He looked about him, 'And where is Ashlyn?'

The final question did it. It all came tumbling out in a flood of tears, the cat and the accident, my mother and the hospital, the interview that should have finished hours ago and Ashlyn's disappearance.

'What makes you think the guy has taken Ashlyn? You know, taking a cat is one thing, she's your pet and he was obviously trying to get to you, but from what you've told me both he and your mother think that Ashlyn is just a student who is lodging with you.'

'From the similarity in our looks and the gap in our ages, Adrian has convinced himself that Ashlyn is my daughter and that you are her father.'

'Bloody hell.' Jared looked stunned and then asked the obvious question, 'Why didn't you just tell him the truth?'

'I haven't told my mother yet and I didn't want to risk her

finding out from Adrian. We should ring the police.' I picked up the phone. 'Will you or shall I?'

'Let's calm down a minute, and give this some thought first.'

I stared at him, 'But Jared, that's just wasting more time and I've wasted enough as it is, meanwhile anything could happen to her.'

'Ashlyn is an eighteen-year-old girl – and a feisty one at that – not a cat to be picked up and carried away. She wouldn't just go off with the guy.'

'Well, no – but he could have fed her a serious line in bull-shit to convince her to go with him.'

'Like?'

I pulled a face, 'Like bad news about my mother, bad news about my cat or about me.'

'She would ring you to check. Ashlyn is nothing if not cautious.'

'My phone was off for most of the time while I was at the hospital. She might have tried and not been able to get through.'

'You've tried her phone, you said.'

'Off and on ever since I got home, she's not answering or picking up her messages either. This is serious, Jared.'

'What about him – the ex?'

'His phone's turned off.'

'OK.' Jared came to a sudden decision. 'This is what we do. We try the ex and then Ashlyn one more time, and if neither one of them answers, we go to his house. If we get no joy there, then we phone the police.'

'I'll make the calls,' I insisted. 'Hearing you might freak

them out – especially Ashlyn if she thinks she's in trouble. If Adrian has her and hears your voice it might prompt him to do something stupid. I can talk to him, calmly and rationally, and convince him to bring her back. If Ashlyn answers I can find out where she is and go and get her.'

Jared agreed, but he looked pretty grim and I didn't much fancy Adrian's chances if it turned out he had taken Ashlyn.

Adrian answered on the first ring of his mobile and I don't know who was more shocked.

'Adrian?'

'Franny? Is that you? How lovely to hear from you. How is Ellie?' he went on in a concerned tone.

'I've been trying to ring you for ages.' I batted away Jared's hand as he tried to take the phone from me, and mouthed, 'Leave this to me'.

'Oh, have you? Yes, the phone's been off most of today. I've been to an important meeting in Scotland. I just flew back into Brankstone Airport.'

I went to speak and he interrupted, 'I thought you'd be impressed. Me, getting on a plane with my fear of flying, but I really couldn't spare the time driving all that way and then back again. I used Ryan Air and in fact it wasn't that bad at all. I might even try going further afield at some point, but listen to me babbling on. I was just so surprised and pleased to hear from you. Does this mean you've forgiven me? I know I behaved like an idiot.' Then he obviously had another thought. 'Oh, please don't tell me that Ellie is...?'

'She's recovering, not thanks to you,' I told him, 'but I just wanted you to know that, and that I still intend to send you the vet's bill. Are you going straight home now?'

'I was. Did you want me to call round?' he asked hopefully.

'No,' I said abruptly and putting the phone down, turned to Jared and told him, 'He doesn't have Ashlyn.'

'And you're sure of that because...?'

'He flew to Scotland today for a meeting and he's only just this minute got back.'

'How can you be so sure of that? The man is an accomplished liar.'

'He sounded absolutely normal, not a hint of anything untoward in his tone and, anyway, we can check the flight times for Ryan Air from Scotland into Brankstone Airport easily enough. You can do that while I ring his secretary. She'll have finished for the day now, but she won't mind me ringing her at home.'

I flipped open my laptop, and left him to it while I picked up the phone again. Without really thinking I tried the office number for Adrian's secretary and though I was more than a little surprised when she picked up the phone it actually helped me to come up with a convincing story.

'Oh, hello, Elaine, it's Francesca. You're working late tonight. I was actually trying to get hold of Adrian but he's not answering his mobile. I thought he might still be at work and that it was worth giving the office a try.'

'He flew up to Scotland for an important meeting this morning – yes, I know, I was surprised he chose to fly as well,' she told me, because although I hadn't said a word we were both well aware of Adrian's aversion to flying. 'I should think,' she went on helpfully, 'that he would be landing back at the local airport right about now, so you should be able to get him shortly.'

'Oh, that's really helpful, Elaine. How are you, and how is that lovely husband of yours?' I listened to her chat about the weekend they had spent in Devon and the holiday they had planned for later in the year. I kept my patience and eventually managed to interrupt. 'Well, I won't keep you. You'll be wanting to get off home.'

'The guy really was in Scotland then, huh?' Jared nodded when I confirmed this, and added, 'I thought so. The flight times match up, too.'

'Where on earth can she be?' I fretted, going to the window to look out onto the darkened and pretty deserted street. 'It's almost 10.30 and the interviews should have finished at three. She could be anywhere, and with anybody, in a strange country. She hardly knows a soul. We should phone the police, right now, Jared.'

'When you say she hardly knows a soul, am I supposed to take that literally? Think about it. Has she made any friends at all?'

'Well, she's on chatting terms with a few of the neighbours,' I mused, and then brightened. 'Do you think she might have gone round to someone's house when she found I wasn't at home, got talking and forgotten all about the time? She might even have thought I would stay at the hospital late and accepted the offer of a meal.'

'Anything is possible,' Jared shrugged. 'Shall we make a start with the ones you know she's friendly with? That's probably what the police would suggest we do.'

Another hour or more passed as we went knocking on

doors that were familiar to me and speaking to the people behind them, who were pretty much strangers. None of them had a bad word to say about Ashlyn and we discovered she had shopped for the elderly, babysat the children and taken in parcels for anyone in full-time employment. Unfortunately, no one had seen her since she'd left to go for her interview, though several commented on how smart she had looked in her suit.

'She promised to let me know how she got on,' they all said and offered to help if a search was organized.

'That's very good of you,' Jared thanked them, 'but I'm sure she'll turn up, probably went for a burger and just forgot the time, you know.' He was trying to sound blasé, but didn't quite pull it off as far as I was concerned.

'You don't think that any more than I do,' I told him as we made our way back to my flat, hurrying a little as we got closer. I knew we were both hoping to find Ashlyn there waiting.

The only sound that greeted us was the sound of Ellie meowing and clawing at the bedroom door in an attempt to get out.

'If you don't ring the police, then I will,' I said, in what I hoped was a firm and no nonsense tone.

Jared still seemed to hesitate and then he came to a decision. 'OK,' he said, 'you try her cell phone one more time and if there's still no answer I'll phone the police. It's nine, nine, nine, in the UK, right?'

At least I didn't have to trawl through a long list of contacts because Ashlyn was right at the top. I pressed 'call' and waited for the answerphone to click in.

I almost dropped the phone when it was answered and a male voice said, 'Are you looking for Ashlyn? Because I have her,' and then the line went dead.

17

'Hello, hello?' I found myself shouting, becoming more frantic by the second, though it was clear whoever had answered Ashlyn's mobile was no longer on the line.

'What is it? What happened?' Jared was beside me in a moment.

'It was a man – on Ashlyn's phone – and he said he has her.'

For the briefest moment Jared looked as stunned as I felt, and then he ordered, 'Ring the number again. Try and find out what he wants. I'm phoning the police.'

My fingers were shaking so much that I fumbled uselessly wasting precious seconds, and then almost dropped my mobile when it rang in my hand and Ashlyn's name again popped up.

All thoughts of remaining calm and reasonable flew out of the window as I pressed the button to take the call and screamed, 'Who are you? What do you want?'

There was only silence for long seconds, then I distinctly heard a soft moan and a fist of fear gripped my heart and squeezed it – hard – but even before I could react, I watched

Ashlyn's name fade from the phone and heard a loud thud against the front door.

My feet refused to move but Jared reacted immediately, racing the few feet to throw the door open wide.

'What the...?' He blasted and swore very loudly.

Rushing to join him it took a moment for my eyes to adjust to the dark outside but in that moment I took in the solid outline of a tall man and, as he stepped forward, I could clearly see the slumped figure of a girl in his arms.

'Ashlyn!' I cried out her name, reached out to touch her and heard the tremble in my voice as I questioned, 'Is she dead?'

'Dead drunk is what she is,' Jared fumed, and, looking ready to punch the guy who was holding her, demanded, 'What the hell were you thinking, bringing her home in this state? She's barely eighteen years old.'

I finally looked at the man, expecting some spotty youth with greasy hair and an attitude problem, and did a double take. 'Lloyd?'

Jared looked from me to Lloyd and then back again. 'You know this guy, right?'

'He lives upstairs. Come on through with her, Lloyd, and let's assess the situation. Where did you find her?' Instinctively, I knew he had nothing to do with Ashlyn's drunken state and hoped my words would convey this to Jared. 'You gave us a fright,' I added, 'when you answered her phone. For a minute we thought she'd been kidnapped when a male voice said he had her.'

'Sorry, I thought I was helping by answering the phone but, as you can see, I had my hands full and had to cut it short. I didn't realize I hadn't said who I was.'

Lloyd put the unconscious figure into an armchair where she slumped, her head lolling onto her chest. It was difficult to see Ashlyn's face for the familiar blonde hair that fell over it in a tangled mess.

'Bloody hell,' I said, looking down at her, 'how on earth did she get into that state?'

'God knows.' Lloyd shrugged his shoulders. 'She was already well gone when I saw her with some student types in one of those pubs in the town centre where you get ten drinks for the price of one or something equally stupid. They were all pretty out of it. I had a bit of trouble persuading her to let me bring her home, but once she passed out the rest was easy.'

'Well, I – we – can't thank you enough, can we, Jared? Jared is Ashlyn's brother,' I added belatedly.

'Sure thing,' Jared offered a hand and the two men shook, as Jared continued, his voice showing clearly how shaken he was, 'God knows what would have happened to her if you hadn't happened along. I really appreciate you getting involved. What happened to the others?'

Lloyd managed a wry grin. 'They weren't in quite the same state – which is just as well because there was no way I could have taken them all home.'

'I can't understand it,' Jared shook his head, 'Ashlyn doesn't drink at home. She never even liked the taste.'

'What are we going to do with her?' I mused. 'That's the question. We can't leave her like this. People can die from alcoholic poisoning or choke on their own vomit. I've read about it often enough in the papers.'

'I wasn't quite sure what to do with her myself,' Lloyd

admitted, 'but there were police around. I didn't want her to get arrested for being drunk and disorderly, so I thought it best to pour her into a taxi and get her home. Though hospital might have been the best thing, in hindsight.'

'We're just so damned grateful you picked her up and got her out of there.' Jared shook his head as he realized out loud, 'Anything could have happened to her.'

'Yes, it could,' I put in. 'What you did was above and beyond the call of duty.'

Lloyd hesitated, and then said, 'Well, I'll leave you to it, if you don't mind. I'll just change my shirt and get back to my friends.'

It was only then I noticed the make up and something that looked suspiciously like vomit stains, smeared over his top.

'I'm so sorry. She's ruined your shirt and your evening.'

'Don't worry about it. I'm just glad I could help. Ashlyn is a lovely kid – when she's sober – and I wouldn't have liked anything to happen to her. I'll pop down and see how she is tomorrow.'

'What a really nice guy,' Jared exclaimed, adding, 'There's not many would have done what he just did, I can tell you.'

'Mmm,' I nodded. 'What are we going to do with her now? We don't know what she's had to drink, or how much? Would she have taken anything, do you think?'

'Taken anything? Drugs, you mean?' Jared shook his head emphatically. 'She doesn't do drugs.'

'You said she didn't drink and she has,' I pointed out. 'Anyway, someone might have spiked her drink.'

While we were staring at Ashlyn, trying to decide what to do for the best, she suddenly lifted her head, peered blearily at us through the tangle of hair, muttered something and promptly threw up. It was only Jared's quick thinking when he thrust a wastepaper bin underneath her chin that averted further disaster as she heaved and heaved until there was nothing left but fresh air.

Wiping her mouth on the back of her sleeve, Ashlyn asked, 'What happened?' and promptly passed out again.

'I think that might just have saved her from the necessity of having her stomach pumped, at least,' I ventured, adding, 'there can't be anything else left.'

'There's still the question of what we do with her now, though.'

I thought about the films and TV dramas I'd seen. 'If you give me a hand we might try getting her under a shower. She's in a right mess and it just might finish sobering her up.'

He didn't demur and getting either side of the chair, we bent down, slung one of her arms around each of our necks and hauled her more or less upright. Ashlyn groaned, and dry retched as we dragged her towards the bathroom. Jared helped me pull off her blouse and the ruined suit. She made only a feeble attempt at fighting us off and once she was propped – still clad in her underwear for modesty's sake – in the corner of the shower stall I stepped in with her with the intention of keeping her upright.

'I can manage now, thanks,' I told him, and closing the door I turned on the water. There was no way I could avoid getting wet, but I kept the icy spray mainly on Ashlyn and it had the desired effect because she seemed to sober up in a minute.

Gasping and spluttering, she yelled, 'What the hell are you doing? Have you gone mad? Leave me alone.'

'Gladly,' I said, dripping water everywhere as I stepped out of the shower stall closing the door firmly behind me. 'Now you just stay in there until you've sobered up. Do you hear me? Your brother and I will have a few well-chosen words to say to you as soon as you're presentable.'

With that I grabbed a towel, sloshed wetly out of the bathroom and started peeling my soaked clothes off the minute I reached my own bedroom. Water ran from my hair and into my eyes, but then I realized the rivulets had been joined by my tears. I really had no idea why I was crying.

Even when I had dried myself off as best I could, pulled on my robe and wrapped my hair in a towel, the tears just would not stop and in the end I gave up and went to join Jared.

He was in the kitchen making the inevitable pot of tea. Turning round to offer me a cup, he immediately put it down and, without hesitation, pulled me into his arms and held me tightly.

'I'm sorry, Fran, so sorry.'

I looked up into his face, into his dark eyes, and couldn't prevent a smile from curving my lips. 'What do you have to be sorry for?'

'We've brought you nothing but grief. You must wish you had never met Mitch's other family.'

'I don't wish that,' I said, and shocked myself by adding, 'but I do wish, very belatedly, that I had met Mitch – my dad – again before he died, if only so that I could find out the truth about our separation.'

'You've still not managed to talk to your mother about it?' Jared had gone back to pouring tea, but he looked at me over his shoulder.

I shook my head. 'Not until we know more about her illness, and perhaps not even then.'

'I admire your patience and tolerance, anyone else would be standing in front of her demanding the truth. I know that I would.'

'I somehow have to accept that she must have acted with the best of intentions because she's not a bad person. She wouldn't have kept us apart simply out of spite over their break-up – of that I am certain.' I watched Jared lift the tray of tea things and then followed him into the sitting room, relieved to see that he had cleaned up and got rid of the bin.

It wasn't very long before the door gave a slight creak and we looked round to see Ashlyn standing there in my old towelling robe, scrubbed clean and looking very young, exceedingly guilty and pretty sorry for herself.

'You're both really angry with me, right?' Her voice was hardly above a whisper and she nodded when neither of us answered. 'I thought you would be, and I don't blame you. I'm not even sure what the hell happened myself in the end but I feel awful.'

'So what happened at the beginning?' Jared's tone was stern, but I thought his mouth twitched, though I might have imagined it.

'Some of the other applicants who were also interviewed today were going for a drink after the interviews and they invited me to go along. I thought that would be fine, you know, because there was no one here to wonder where I was.'

If she was trying to make me feel guilty Ashlyn was making a good job of it, but she knew I'd had no choice and that's what I told her in no uncertain terms, reminding her of exactly why I hadn't been at home.

'Oh, I know that. How is your mum? Do you know anything yet?' When I shook my head, she continued, 'I only meant it to be one drink, and then I was going to come home and make a meal, but before I knew it I'd had two or three and then it all became a blur.'

'It usually does when you get drunk,' Jared pointed out.

'But it only tasted like lemonade.'

'Probably those alco-pop thingies,' I nodded. 'I've heard some of them can be lethal.'

'Why aren't you both shouting at me? And why are you even here, Jared? You didn't say you were coming over.'

'Thought I'd surprise you and ask in person how the interview went. Instead you managed to surprise us by disappearing off the face of the earth. Do you know how worried we've been, Ashlyn? Francesca didn't need all this, today of all days.'

'And why weren't you answering your phone?' I put in, 'I've been ringing ever since I left the hospital and pretty continually since I got home.'

'I didn't hear it ring,' Ashlyn looked puzzled and then smacked her hand against her forehead and said, 'I put it on silent when I got to the university and then forgot all about it. I'm so sorry, really I am.'

'Well, at least you're safe.' I suddenly couldn't see the point of going on and on, but I still couldn't resist adding, 'But it could have been an entirely different story if Lloyd hadn't practically scraped you up off the floor and poured you into a taxi. You'll have to thank him and apologize, because he was on an evening out with friends when he saw you and came to your rescue.'

'I feel terrible,' Ashlyn wailed.

'And so you should,' Jared told her sternly.

'No, I mean it, I do feel terrible,' and with a hand clamped to her mouth Ashlyn ran off in the direction of the bathroom and slammed the door behind her.

'I don't think she'll be doing that again in a hurry,' he said, with some satisfaction. 'She might just have learned her lesson.'

It was late, I was exhausted both mentally and physically and, I suddenly realized, also starving hungry. It had been a long and emotionally draining day.

'I'm making some toast,' I declared suddenly, knowing I wasn't up to conjuring up even the simplest of meals at that time of night. I didn't wait for Jared to reply, but realized he was right behind me as I made my way to the kitchen.

Fresh tea was made to go with toast that was spread thickly with butter the minute it popped out of the toaster.

'Mmm,' we murmured, nodding at each other in appreciative agreement, ignoring the jam, marmalade and cream cheese I had placed on the table.

Eventually Ashlyn joined us, even managing a dry piece of toast, and eventually she was able to tell us about her day – prior to the drinking session.

'What did you think of the university?' was my question. 'You know, the people, the place?'

'The place could have done with a lick of paint,' Ashlyn

commented. 'You know how it is, with scuffs here and there, and marks on the carpet where drinks had been spilt. But you couldn't fault the people. Kathryn Horne was just as friendly face-to-face as she was on the phone. She was there to collect our photos.'

'Was everyone on time?' was Jared's question, which I thought was a bit random.

'Well, no,' Ashlyn shook her head. 'We had to be there at ten o'clock, and most of us were early, but a few did wander in late – some didn't even apologize, which I thought was a bit rude. It gave the impression they didn't give a shit. Excuse me.' She put a hand over her mouth. 'Anyway, they missed some of the talk, which was about an hour long. We got to meet some current students, which was great, and then each had an individual interview. It was all over by three o'clock.'

'How do you think it went?' Jared and I asked the same question at the same time and smiled at each other before turning our attention back to Ashlyn.

She pulled a face. 'Hard to tell, the interviewers – there were three – were very friendly, but they were probably the same with everyone. They asked a lot of questions about my background and experience and I think I gave a good account of myself.'

'When will they make a decision?' I asked, and found myself wondering what would happen if Ashlyn was unsuccessful. Would she go back to her old life in Canada and would I – could I – go back to my old life?

18

Later still, I lay beside my sister, watching her sleep surprisingly peacefully after her ordeal, knowing that Jared – the man who was her brother but unrelated to me – was sleeping in my bed on the other side of the wall.

I wondered if I had finally come to some understanding of what a family was, and to accept that it could come in all manner of guises. The realization came that I might have wasted the majority of my life so far wishing to be a part of the *ideal* family when, in all probability there was no such thing.

The majority of families in modern times were like this family of mine and made up of a combination of what had always been thought of as traditional – two parents married or unmarried but with children only from that union – except often added into the mix were step-parents and step- and half-siblings. Whatever the mix, the result was still a family and the glue that held most together was love, usually with a dash of common sense and mutual respect.

A flash of sudden perception told me I could waste more time regretting – not only the years of not knowing I had a sister, but also the time I might have spent with my father

– knowing all the regrets in the world wouldn't change the past. It was only in my power to change the future and the future started with the present moment. I understood I was also going to have to deal with my mother and her deception, but that could only happen when the time was right. I might also try and understand that she probably had regrets of her own.

I smoothed the tangle of blonde hair back from Ashlyn's youthful face and was grateful for the determination to get to know more about me that had sent her on the long journey to a strange land. The dissimilarity in our ages and backgrounds really didn't seem very important any more, just that against the odds we had come together and been given the chance to make our relationship become all the things that it always should have been.

'Thank you,' I whispered, and couldn't help smiling when Ashlyn's eyes opened briefly and she said, ''S all right,' without having a clue what I might have been thanking her for, before closing them again and drifting back to sleep.

At some point I must have drifted off to sleep as well and I woke alone. The sun was streaming into a room that wasn't my usual bedroom, so that I felt disorientated for a moment or two and was left wondering what on earth I was doing in there. Memories of the night before filtered through slowly and the realization that it could have turned out very differently if it hadn't been for Lloyd's swift actions made me feel slightly sick and cross with myself for allowing it to happen. Though how I could actually have prevented any of it was quite beyond me, since I had not yet discovered the secret to being in two places at one and the same time.

I swung my feet out of bed and reached for the old robe that Ashlyn normally used as her own. I don't know what I was expecting to find when I opened the kitchen door, but it definitely wasn't Ashlyn looking bright-eyed and bushy-tailed – just as if the night before had never happened – serving breakfast to a smiling Jared, who had been joined at the table by an equally amiable Lloyd.

They were all dressed for the day ahead and I felt at a distinct disadvantage. The thoughts uppermost in my mind were that without make-up I always looked totally washed out and the realization that I should at least have taken the time to brush the tangles out of my hair. I found myself pushing it self-consciously out of my eyes and smoothing the towelling folds of the shabby bathrobe in a ridiculous and ineffectual attempt to tidy myself.

Ushered to a chair by Jared, a heaped plate of bacon, egg and God knows what else was place in front of me by a decidedly sheepish Ashlyn, while toast was offered and tea poured by Lloyd.

'I can't eat all of that,' I protested, when I realized they were all looking at me expectantly. 'I rarely eat more than a piece of toast.'

'Just do your best,' Ashlyn encouraged, 'please.'

'Have you…?' I began.

'Apologized to Lloyd?' the sheepish look was firmly back in place. 'Yes, I have, over and over again, and I want to do the same to you, but just want you to enjoy your food first, you know.'

Lloyd was nodding encouragingly, as was Jared, so I cut a small piece of bacon and as I chewed, realized I was actually starving hungry and tucked right in, completely forgetting to mind that they were all watching me.

Only when two slices of toast and marmalade had followed the full English, and I was sipping a fresh cup of tea, did Ashlyn attempt her apology, stumbling in her efforts to make each word count and to make me understand how truly sorry she was.

'I accept, totally, that I have ruined any chance of living with you for the next three years, but if we can just be friends—'

'No,' I said firmly and emphatically. I watched Ashlyn's face fall and her shoulders droop, and then I went swiftly on, 'we can never "just be friends", because we are so much more. We are sisters and we are family and – providing you weren't planning on taking part in regular pub crawls – it would be my great pleasure to have you living with me for the next three years.'

There was a stunned silence, and I found myself as silent as the rest when I belatedly realized the importance of Ashlyn's words.

'You've been offered a place on the course.' It was a statement, not a question, and I leapt to my feet, uncaring that my cup had overturned and tea was dripping onto the floor.

'You want me to stay, even after everything, right?'

'Yes,' I said.

'Yes,' Ashlyn said, and launched herself at me right across the room and knocked the breath right out of me.

'That's a bit of a result all round, then,' Lloyd grinned, and we all laughed out loud.

There followed a flurry of questions and answers, more

apologies, more hugs and congratulations and a decision was reached to celebrate in some way while Jared was still in the country to join in.

Caught up in the excitement we threw suggestions around as to the form the celebration might take, until Lloyd suddenly exclaimed, 'Is that the time? I'd better take myself off to work.' He paused in the doorway, 'What about a having a barbeque in the garden? That wouldn't take too much organizing and the weather is great right now.'

'Good idea,' I approved, accepting without question that he would be joining us because without his timely intervention there would have been no celebration. 'Meanwhile, you should ring your mother, Ashlyn, if you haven't already.' I suddenly stopped talking and clapped a hand to my mouth. 'Oh, my God, what about *my* mother? With all that's happened I haven't given her a thought. How terrible is that? I must get ready and get myself off to the hospital. She'll be going home today.'

'We'll clear up, won't we, Jared?' Ashlyn offered immediately, ushering me towards the door, 'and you can leave preparations for the barbeque to Jared and me. We have them all the time at home. You take a shower and get ready. Should I come with you?' She shook her head immediately, 'Oh, no, stupid idea right?'

'It's not a stupid idea.' I patted her arm. 'I do want the two of you to meet, but not right now. I think my mother has enough to deal with for the moment.'

'Sure,' she agreed immediately.

*

Roy was already at the hospital, fussing around my mother and chivvying her along. He may well have started the day grimly determined to be positive and encouraging in his approach, but by the time I got there both patience and optimism appeared to be wearing thin. On the whole he was just being his usual bossy self. I could hear him issuing orders before I even walked into the ward.

My mother looked pale and uncomfortable, holding her arm carefully and looking as if she wished herself elsewhere. She looked relieved to see me. 'Oh, there you are, Franny,' she greeted me, the cheerful tone forced.

'About time, too,' Roy grumbled, 'we were beginning to wonder how we would manage, because your mother is insisting she can't walk to the entrance on her own, and I have all these bags to manage.'

I looked pointedly at the two bags he was making such a fuss about, but carefully held my tongue.

'I'm here now,' I said in what I hoped was a soothing voice, and turning to my mother, I added, 'we can get a wheelchair if it will help, Mum. I'm sure no one will mind.'

'Oh, I don't think that will be necessary, there's nothing wrong with her legs,' Roy sounded horrified at the suggestion, but my mother just looked relieved and whispered, 'Thank you, Franny.'

I knew we would be back in a week for the results, but it was still a relief to get outside of a building full of sick and dying people. I knew it was a ridiculous way to feel and reminded myself firmly that it was also the place where people went to be made well. I guessed it was a fear of the unknown, because I'd never had so much as a tonsil removed in my life and to someone like me even a trip to the dentist was traumatic. It was pathetic and I told myself in strong terms to think of my mother and how she might be feeling.

She seemed loath to let me go even when she was in her own home and tucked up in her own bed. We had been warned she would be a bit sore and tired, but she seemed weepy and emotional, too, and kept a tight hold on my hand.

I could tell Roy didn't like this sudden dependence on me, as he constantly reminded my mother that I had a job to go to and she mustn't make demands on my time. I was used to him and his need to be number one in my mother's life. It was one of the things that had affected my relationship, effectively driving a wedge between us, but this time I wasn't prepared to allow him to shut me out.

'I'll stay for as long as Mum needs me,' I said, my tone firm, 'Temping work is just what it says it is – temporary – and the recruitment agency I work for have been very understanding, given my long record of reliability.'

We sat quietly, but Roy fussed with the covers, with the pillows, continually tidying what didn't need to be tidied, doing anything that made him appear indispensable to my mother's needs until she said, through gritted teeth, 'Could you make us some tea, Roy dear, and use the good china, please?'

He looked absolutely torn between a strong desire to please his sick wife, and his grim determination to ensure we weren't left alone in case we became too close in his absence. In the end he had no choice and he knew it.

'I won't be long,' he said with a warning look that made me

wonder if he really thought I had it in my mind to make off with my mother while he was gone.

I said nothing but wondered how on earth she put up with him.

'He means well,' my mother defended him, as if she had read my mind.

I'd heard myself excuse Adrian in the same way many times over the years of our marriage, but it was only in that moment that I realized how alike he and Roy were. The difference was, it obviously suited my mother to be loved so possessively and exclusively that she rarely made a decision, and scarcely made a move without Roy by her side. For my part, I had simply woken up one morning and realized that if I didn't leave I was going to suffocate.

'I'm sure he does,' I agreed.

'We all mean well,' she murmured tiredly. 'We do our best.'

'Of course we do,' I soothed, intent on keeping my mother calm and hoping she would sleep because she so obviously needed to.

'We make our choices,' she went on, turning her head on the pillow to look straight at me, 'and we can only hope they are the right ones, for everyone concerned, but how can we really know?'

I stared at her, wondering what she was getting at and then the next minute wondering if she was saying what I thought she was saying.

'Is there something you want to talk about, Mum?' I asked trying to keep the urgency I was beginning to feel out of my voice.

She nodded slowly, and said chillingly, 'Yes, there is, before it's too late. I should have talked to you years ago but you were just a child and then it never seemed like quite the right time to bring it all up. I always thought there was plenty of time. You never mentioned him, it was as if you had forgotten....'

Very gently, I asked her, 'Is this about my father?'

We both jumped as Roy's voice rang harshly from the doorway. 'Your father?' he demanded, 'Your father? *I'm* the only father you've known, the one who brought you up and the only one you remember. Now, you're upsetting your mother. You should know better than that after what she's just gone through. I think it's time you left.'

19

I left. There was nothing else I could do with my poor mother looking so frail and close to tears and the overbearing Roy standing over her like a lioness protecting its cub, but I was left desperately wondering what she had been going to tell me. For the moment I was no closer to knowing if it might have been the truth about my father's absence from my life, at last, or merely some watered down version meant to appease me and go some way to clearing her conscience.

My head was spinning with the things I already knew and what I might have discovered. When I got home to find preparations for a celebration barbeque were in full swing, it took me a few moments to recall what, exactly, we were celebrating. I certainly hadn't expected it to be organized so quickly.

'Are you OK?' Jared paused in the self-imposed task of scrubbing potatoes ready for baking and gave me a straight look.

I shook my head to rid it of the questions that buzzed round and round like angry wasps trapped in a jam jar.

'Is it your mum?' he wiped his hands on a tea towel and

came over to me. 'You're worried about her. We should have thought, you probably don't want all this going on right now.' Putting his hands on my shoulders he looked into my eyes, his face a picture of concern.

'No, it's fine. She's fine for now. Who knows what the future holds for her? There is no point worrying meanwhile and she's in safe hands. We won't know any more for a few days yet and this is probably just what I need to take my mind off things. What can I do to help?'

In fact, I quickly came to realize it was exactly what I needed, and just what I had always wanted – without ever knowing what that was. Finding myself part of a family, surrounded by friends and enjoying the kind of social life that other people took for granted was something I used to imagine through the lonely years of a childhood and marriage spent putting my own wishes last. As smiling people I had only ever passed in the street came through my front door carrying bottles of wine and beer or bowls of crisp salad, rice mixture and coleslaw, I felt my spirits lift in spite of everything.

Following them through to the garden I was surprised to see there were already portable barbeques in place with the coals beginning to glow red, each tended by neighbours I vaguely recognized. Before long the smell of meat cooking had queues eagerly forming, plates at the ready. My very first taste of a beefburger in a bun smothered in fried onion and tomato sauce was probably the best thing I had ever tasted in my life – or so it seemed as I stood enjoying the food and the company.

Everyone seemed to know everyone else and it made me

wonder why I had continued to isolate myself even after Adrian's controlling influence was gone from my life. I hadn't exactly snubbed my neighbours but neither had I gone out of my way to be friendly in the time I had lived on the street. There was no doubt my father leaving when I was four years old had a profound effect on my life but even I was finally beginning to realize I couldn't keep blaming him, or Adrian either, for what was still wrong with my life. It was time to start letting go of the past and taking some responsibility for my own happiness.

It was surprisingly easy to be sociable, I found, because though old habits died hard and I had never been comfortable talking about myself, most people appeared to be happy to talk freely about themselves if you showed an interest in them, their lives and their loved ones.

Lloyd seemed to prove this point when he came to stand beside me and immediately asked, 'How's Ellie?' Tall and tanned, with the physique of a builder, he was drinking beer straight from the bottle – as indeed were most of the men and some of the woman. Realizing how horrified Adrian would have been almost made me giggle.

I smiled up at him. 'She's fine and still has eight lives left, thanks to you. There she is, look,' I pointed to my bedroom window and said ruefully, 'furious to be kept inside and making a good job of shredding my curtains, which is a small price to pay. Without you I might have found myself without a cat – and even worse, without a sister.'

'I only realized recently that Ashlyn was your sister,' he commented.

My newfound confidence allowed me to admit, 'I only realized quite recently that I *had* a sister and it's taking a bit of getting used to. I didn't know my father had even remarried because we had lost touch so it came as quite a shock, I can tell you. Jared is not my brother, of course.'

Lloyd took another a sip of his beer. 'No, I gathered that. Are you two a couple?'

'No.' I was stunned that he might think so, and then stunned to find that I quite liked the idea that we might be. I had obviously been alone too long and quickly reminded myself that he was almost a brother to me – but there was no denying that he was no such thing and we weren't related at all.

Someone called Lloyd away then, and I found myself watching Jared across the garden. He was easy to spot, being so tall, as he made his way easily from one group to the next, chatting and laughing in that easy way he and Ashlyn shared and that I so envied. He looked up suddenly and caught me looking at him. Embarrassed I went to turn away, but when he came over bringing wine for me in a stemmed plastic glass, Ashlyn joined us and any awkwardness on my part disappeared. She was sipping what looked like orange juice and I found myself sincerely hoping that was *all* there was in the tumbler.

Catching my glance and interpreting it correctly, she laughed, held up the drink and assured me, 'It *is* only juice. No more alcohol for me, I've only just stopped feeling queasy. I've definitely learned my lesson.'

Laughing, I gave her a hug, and Jared joined in the laughter, and said, 'I certainly hope so. Clearing up behind you almost made me teetotal,' which set us all off again.

'Oh, that's nice that is,' said a hatefully familiar voice behind me. 'What a cosy little picture – you ought to get it framed. What did I tell you, Roy? You can't deny the evidence of your own eyes, can you?'

I turned slowly and came face to face with my ex-husband and my stepfather. The similarity of the sneering expressions on their faces might have been comical in any other situation.

'How did you get in here – you have no business just turning up at my home uninvited.'

I was uncomfortably conscious that everyone in the garden had gradually stopped talking and all eyes were on us, obviously wondering what was going on.

'And all these people are here by invitation,' Adrian hazarded a guess, his confidence bolstered by the belligerent presence of my stepfather, 'to celebrate what – your engagement? About eighteen years too late in my estimation.' He turned and asked, 'Was I right, Roy, or was I right? There's no denying they're mother and daughter, like two peas in a pod, and he—' Adrian thrust a finger in Jared's direction – 'is quite obviously the father. I knew it when I saw them all together in that restaurant. I bet Francesca's own mother doesn't even know that Francesca has a child. I certainly didn't and I,' he told the silent crowd, 'am her husband.'

Once upon a time, not too long ago, I might have shrivelled up from embarrassment and allowed him to shred my reputation unhindered but, as I had so recently decided, it was time for me to take responsibility. I drew myself up to my full height and prepared to stand up for myself.

'You,' I stated loudly and clearly, pointing a finger of my

own until it was practically touching Adrian's stunned face, 'are my *ex*-husband. This,' I lowered my hand and reached behind me to draw Ashlyn forward, 'is my *sister*. Do you hear that, Adrian? Ashlyn is my *sister* and Jared is her *brother*. Now, I suggest you make at least a bit of an effort to get your facts straight before you throw around accusations in future.'

'Hear, hear,' muttered one of my neighbours and it was followed by a clear murmur of agreement from a good few of the others.

'I – uh, you never said, never told me,' Adrian stammered.

'And that,' I said very precisely, 'is because you are my *ex*-husband, no longer part of my life and no longer entitled to know everything about me. It was a mistake on my part to ever think we could remain friends. It is a mistake I will not be repeating. Now, please get off my premises and out of my life – and stay out of it.'

He left without another word, but I was pleased that Roy showed no inclination to follow him. I think he was shocked and not very impressed by Adrian's spiteful behaviour.

'Please carry on,' I urged everyone. 'You came to celebrate Ashlyn's achievement with us and I'm very glad that you did. My stepfather and I need to have a little chat, but it won't take long. Take care of everyone, Jared, Ashlyn, and I'll be right back.'

Everyone was outside in the garden; the house was empty, so I took Roy through to the sitting room and sat him down, offering, 'Can I get you tea, Roy? Coffee or something stronger?'

'You can tell me what the hell is going on,' he said. His

voice was hoarse as if he'd only just found it again after being lost for words for a while.

'What else can I tell you?' I queried, 'probably not very much because you, of all people, must know that my mother has kept in touch with my biological father all these years.'

He looked as if I had slapped him and I realized almost immediately that I had just made a serious error of judgement by assuming my mother had shared her secret with him. It was clear from his stunned expression that she had not. I took a deep breath, realizing it was far too late to stop now.

'I don't think it was a two way thing,' I offered, 'I only found out there was any contact at all because he died quite recently and among his effects there were photos of me. From when I was a small child and right up to these last few years there were pictures of me – at school, on holiday, when I was confirmed, when I was married, and letters, too – in my mother's handwriting.'

'What did she say in the letters?' Roy was shaking his head in disbelief – at his own wife's behaviour, I imagined, because he clearly didn't disbelieve what I was telling him. Even he must realize there was absolutely no reason for me to lie about such a thing.

'I don't know,' I told him. 'I never read them, because I wanted to hear the truth from my mother's own lips. Can you blame me? She chose to keep his whereabouts and his interest in me from me and I don't even know why.' Again he shook his head, and I continued, 'She must have had her reasons and I needed to know what those reasons were but, before I had the chance to ask her about any of this, she told me about the cancer scare. I knew then that, even after all these years it still wasn't the right time for me to insist on hearing the truth.'

He looked upset and obviously found it difficult to ask, 'Earlier, with your mother when I asked you to leave, you didn't start that conversation, did you?'

I shook my head. 'It's been so long I was prepared to wait a bit longer but Mum brought the subject up. While you were out of the room she said something like, "I should have talked to you years ago but it never seemed like quite the right time to bring it all up and I always thought there was plenty of time. You never mentioned him, it was as if you had forgotten...." That was when I asked her, "Is this about my father?" and then you came in.'

'I only caught the tail end, heard you say, "about my father," and I thought you were plaguing. If I'm being honest I was jealous and also upset that either of you would want to even bother to mention the man who deserted you both all those years ago. I should have understood that he gave you life and will always be your father. How can I compete with that?'

I'd never heard Roy be so honest, and I reached out to touch his hand. 'You did your best and I've always appreciated that, but it was my mother you married and I came as part of the package. She was obviously always your priority and you were so close as a couple that I was never sure where exactly I fitted in; as a result I was often a very lonely child. That being the case, is it any wonder I became almost obsessed with the father who left me at such a young age and why that might have been?'

He looked as if he was about to burst into tears. 'I don't think I've ever thought about it from your point of view until now,' he said ruefully. 'It suited me to pretend he never existed and it seemed to suit your mother, too.'

'Do you know anything about him or why he left?' I asked the question hopefully, but thought I already knew the answer.

Roy shook his head, 'Joan told me no more than she obviously ever told you. Precisely nothing. Not that I was interested in a man who could just up and walk away from his family and I've always assumed that was the case. Thinking back,' he admitted, 'I probably made it too difficult for her confide in me, even if she wanted to – I've always been a very jealous man. Even jealous of you – Joan's own child – if I'm honest, and I realize that's a terrible thing to say. I did always want my wife to myself.'

I tried to be generous and said, 'I've no doubt you had your reasons, just as my mother obviously has hers.'

He shrugged, 'Mine were coming from a large family with little love to go round, I expect, but you'd have thought that would make me more sensitive to the needs of a child, not less. I've always been fond of you, but I realize now that I could have showed it a lot more. If you want to come and talk to your mother about all of this, I promise not to interfere. Whether Joan chooses to discuss it with *me* at any point will be entirely her decision, I can live without knowing, but I can fully accept now that it's high time you knew the truth.'

'I would prefer that to making up my own version of events as Adrian seems to have done.' I had a sudden thought, 'Did he just turn up at the house?'

'Yes,' Roy looked suddenly furious, 'but luckily Joan was asleep and I insisted we didn't wake her. God knows what she would have made of his little story. Hopefully, she hasn't missed me, but I asked a neighbour to sit with her while I came here. I take it she doesn't know about your father's other family?'

'I have no idea,' I said flatly, 'no idea at all. I don't even know if she's aware that he died recently.'

He was obviously taken aback. 'I didn't realize and I really am very sorry, Franny.' I thought it was the first time since he came into my life that he had ever called me by my pet name. 'I hope your mother confides in you soon. It's the least you deserve after all these years, but I don't think that you will have much longer to wait. I shall say nothing to Joan about what you've told me tonight because this is between the two of you.'

After Roy left I made a huge effort and went back to the party that had resumed outside. This went against my usual behaviour, which would have been to avoid dealing with the result of such a public confrontation at all costs.

Over the years I'd lost count of the number of jobs I had left immediately after one of Adrian's embarrassing altercations until I gave up and became a temp; the number of friends I had found it too difficult to face, so that it just seemed easier to walk away and cut all ties than to try and explain. Too afraid to insist that my husband face up to his actions in case he left me – until I'd finally accepted that I was far lonelier with him that I would ever be without him. Those days were over and I was prepared only to accept responsibility for my own actions and words and no one else's.

I expected everyone to ignore the situation – which is exactly what I would have done in the past but, while making it clear that I could talk of the matter or not as I chose, others were quick to share their experiences of a difficult family life with me. I was quite astonished how many felt able to share similar situations to my own through their lives. Dysfunctional families were obviously a fact of life for many and so many words of wisdom were shared that I felt I should get a notebook and jot them down.

'It's easy to blame yourself for the actions of others, but you must ask yourself what choice you had.'

'It's important not to look back with regret. We cannot change the past, only the future.'

'We can't change the behaviour of others – only our own.'

Everyone was so kind, assuring me they would be looking out for me, that their doors were always open and I must never feel alone. All those people I had previously passed in the street, seeing them only as uncaring strangers, had actually been friends in the making, but it had taken Ashlyn with her open mind and heart to show me that.

I made a little speech saying as much, and we raised our plastic glasses to Ashlyn, wishing her luck with her chosen university course in the months ahead.

Within minutes of the last person leaving, with the sky growing light, Roy arrived back on my doorstep to tell me, 'Your mother is asking to see you,' and I knew the years of waiting to hear the truth about my father were finally over.

20

Roy refused to elaborate much beyond assuring me that my mother knew nothing at all about Adrian turning up or that Roy had been with him to see me.

'She simply woke very early in a great state of agitation and said she had to speak to you. I think she was surprised when I didn't object or question her – as we all know I normally would have.' Roy looked embarrassed.

'You want Fran to go with you now, right?' Ashlyn looked worried.

'She's had no sleep,' Jared pointed out, 'can't it wait?'

'I couldn't sleep if I wanted to now and after waiting so long for this moment, I don't want to wait another second longer than I have to. Go to bed, both of you and I will see you soon.'

Roy insisted on driving me to their house, and though I'd had very little to drink I was glad to have the opportunity to gather my chaotic thoughts into some kind of order. We were mostly silent beyond me asking how my mother had seemed when he'd left and receiving the assurance that she had 'seemed calm and just said she was ready to be straight with you'.

When we arrived I felt a strange reluctance to leave the car and go into the house. Despite my previous eagerness to get to the truth, I felt disinclined to hurry up the stairs, almost having to force myself to the top and through the open doorway where my mother sat bolt upright in the wide bed. She looked very frail and, frankly, terrified.

I walked across and took both of her hands in mine. They were ice cold. 'How are you?' I asked, and managed to smile encouragingly, 'and what's all this about?'

'I don't know where to start,' she said, and promptly burst noisily into tears that were verging on the hysterical.

I knew Roy would be nearby and would have heard how upset she was. I half expected him to come crashing through the door, telling me to look at what I'd done and ordering me out, and was relieved and impressed when he did no such thing. Catching the faint clink of china and cutlery I guessed he was busying himself making tea down in the kitchen, obviously determined to leave us to it.

'The beginning,' I suggested, and she managed a watery smile and patting the bed beside her, invited me to, 'Come and sit here'.

'Do you want Roy to be here?' I felt I should offer.

'No,' she said firmly, 'this is between you and me. I can talk to him later.'

The story was a common one of the times. It was the sixties and she and my father were young and fancied themselves in love; teenage lust soon resulted in an unwanted pregnancy. In those days and in those cases there was still a lot of parental pressure on youngsters in that situation to marry and opt for respectability and my parents bowed to the pressure to 'do the right thing'.

It was different then, my mother explained; there weren't the benefits available to top up low wages. My father was working for a small local builder and trying to learn a trade, while my mother coped with a small baby in a scruffy flat with three flights of stairs to climb. The lack of money and freedom was difficult to cope with.

'It wasn't what either of us had expected or wanted,' my mother told me honestly. 'We scarcely knew each other despite having a child and were just kids playing at being grown-ups really, but we did both love you.'

'I know,' I said.

My mother looked at me in astonishment, 'You remember?'

'Yes,' I nodded, 'I remember.'

'But you were so young, when he—'

'I remember,' I repeated firmly.

'Mitchell was offered a job overseas – in Canada,' she picked up the story again, mentioning my father's name for the first time. 'I can't remember who by, or why, but I remember him being so excited and talking of a new start. I always had my doubts, but he had everything planned and was to go first and send for us when he was settled in his new job and had a home for us to go to. I suppose I allowed myself to get carried away by his enthusiasm.

'He cried when he left us, and promised that it wouldn't be for long. Nothing seemed to go right, though, and it took a lot longer than we first thought. By the time he had everything ready for us I had got used to living without him and so had you. It seemed so far away and we had our own life here.

Telling him I had changed my mind was the hardest thing I ever had to do but I had to do what was right for me.'

'What about me?'

'Well, of course, what was right for you, too. You were settled in school by then. We decided it would be best altogether if it was a clean break now that he had his life out there.'

'Who decided?'

'What?' my mother stared at me.

'Who decided a clean break would be best?'

She hesitated, but I persisted, 'Who?'

'I did,' she admitted, finally and suddenly.

'That the clean break would be best for whom exactly?'

'Well, you – less confusing – you were only young.'

'Old enough to know there was a daddy-shaped hole in my life. Old enough to think he didn't love me any more.' I could hear the anguish in my voice and I made no attempt to hide it. 'I spent my life wondering where he was and why he had left.'

'But you never said anything.' My mother looked startled, confused. 'Never asked about him. I thought you had forgotten.'

'You *hoped* I had forgotten. By refusing to talk about him yourself and getting upset when I tried, you made me afraid to persist in case you left me too, and therefore ensured that all trace of my father was erased from my life. I can't believe you thought I wouldn't find that confusing.'

'You had me, and eventually you had Roy,' she protested.

'I had a father of my own, but was denied the right to know and love him.'

'You've been an adult for a long time,' my mother reminded me, suddenly placing the responsibility firmly back with me, 'and could either have insisted I tell you what I knew or tried to trace Mitchell yourself.'

'Agreed,' I nodded, 'but I thought he had left me, remember, and that he had made the choice not to keep in touch. I thought he had no interest in me, but that wasn't exactly true, was it?'

'What do you mean?'

'He knew all about my life here from letters and photos that had been sent to him, going back years. Letters and photos sent to him by you.'

This time when my mother burst into tears, Roy did come in but he was carrying the tea tray and he didn't rush to her side.

'It's time for the truth, Joan.' His tone was gentle and encouraging, I could detect no trace of anger. 'I think it's something we both deserve to be told.'

'All right,' she said, 'all right. I made the decision that a clean break was best, because my father left me, too, when I was quite small.'

I gaped at her because I had been given the impression my maternal grandfather was dead and since his name was never mentioned in my hearing, had assumed it pained my mother to talk about him. History, it seemed, did repeat itself.

'However,' she continued, 'unlike your father, he would turn up out of the blue at infrequent intervals – only to leave again. He would be there when I left for school in the morning, and be gone by the time I returned home. His comings and goings disrupted the whole of my childhood and I just didn't want that for you.

'And my father agreed?'

'We both just wanted to do what was best for you, but to say he was reluctant to lose all contact is an understatement. So we made a compromise, and all of the contact came from me with regular reports on your progress, together with photographs. It wasn't a two-way thing. To be honest, I'm surprised he kept his side of the bargain so long and didn't try to get in touch.'

'Are you?' I said sadly, trying very hard to understand it from her point of view. 'When I didn't bother to try and get in touch with him he probably thought I had forgotten all about him, just as I assumed he had forgotten about me.'

'I'm so sorry.' Tears trickled down my mother's face, and she was so pale that I was worried about her in spite of myself. 'I was very wrong to keep you apart but it's only now that I can see the damage I've done.' Then she brightened considerably. 'I still have his contact details, and even after all this time it's not too late.'

I almost felt sorry for her as I said as gently as I could, 'It is too late, I'm afraid. My father is dead.'

21

It became all too much for both of us, and I left soon after. Assuring my mother I held nothing against her, and accepting she felt she had acted for the best, wasn't easy and in other circumstances I might well have let my bitter resentment show.

Bowing to the pleading look in Roy's eyes, I insisted, 'What's done is done,' in an effort to calm her down, 'you were only trying to protect me as any mother would.'

In fact, I found it hard to accept that was true. My mother might have convinced herself she'd made the decisions she had with what was best for me in mind, but I was far from being convinced that she hadn't actually done what was best and easiest for her.

It was clear to me she didn't fully understand the way her actions in my childhood had influenced my own through the years. Even her choice of a second husband had influenced my choice of a partner because in taking Roy as a model of dependability I had mistaken jealousy and possessiveness for love; controlling for caring. The kind of marriage that had suited my mother had, in the end, threatened to smother me.

Roy was unexpectedly understanding, saying as he showed me out of the house, 'I can appreciate how you feel and I totally agree that the truth should have been told right from the start, but perhaps try and see it from your mother's point of view, hmmm?'

I nodded, and pulled a face, 'I am trying, Roy, I promise you, but it's not easy when I can't vent my anger on either of my parents for the decisions they made – because one is ill and the other is dead.'

I had refused his offer of a lift home, needing to walk in the fresh air in an effort to clear my head. The streets were busy as the town came to life and looking into the face of each passer-by I wondered what stories they might have to tell. As I walked I even came to accept that my own was not so unusual and that many would have had to come to terms with worse things than an absent parent. It was probably about time I did the same – the problem was that I didn't know where to start.

In the end, following a phone call, I was persuaded to cross the miles to Canada again in my search for answers.

Jared had returned home with Ashlyn in order for them to have some family time together prior to her starting the course at Brankstone University. I missed them both and, at the sound of his voice I felt my spirits lift until I heard what he had to say.

'Mitchell Browning's will,' my tone was sharp, as I added, 'what has that to do with me?'

'You are a beneficiary, Fran. Surely you can't be surprised? You were, after all, Mitch's daughter.'

'Not in any way that counted,' I said firmly, 'I have no need of his money.' I almost added that all I had ever wanted was his love, but I had a feeling Jared already knew that because he had often appeared to understand as no one else ever had.

'Whatever you decide,' Jared said softly, 'you should be here when the will is read. Who knows, hearing your father's last wishes might help you to understand the man and his actions and enable you to put the past to rest. If you come back for no other reason, it would be good for Ashlyn to have you by her side at such a time.'

'I have to be by my mother's side when she gets her results, and if it's bad news ...' my voice tailed off.

'It could equally be good news,' he pointed out and I took comfort from the truth of that simple statement. 'The date for the reading can be arranged to suit you. Why not stay on for a while, make a proper holiday of it this time and see something of Canada? We would love to have you here. You never know, you might even decide to make your home here one day.'

I wondered then if I was imagining the growing attraction between us or if he felt it too and I shivered. I tried reminding myself that he was just trying to make me feel welcome, but it was no use because the seed had already been sown.

In fact, it was good news from the hospital, and sitting with my mother as she was told all the cancerous cells had been removed during the lumpectomy and that the lymph nodes were clear, relief flooded through me. She obviously thought that was all there was to it and had already reached for her handbag, preparing to go and share the good news with Roy.

We had left him pacing the corridor outside after he'd declared that I would be much better in the support role than he would ever be. For a big strong man, I sometimes found him exceptionally weak and it was difficult not to be judgemental.

'However,' the consultant said, and my mother's hands returned to her lap, clasped together so tightly that the knuckles were white. I reached over and covered them with one of mine, giving what I hoped was a comforting squeeze. I imagined that my eyes would be as wide and scared as I could see my mother's were as we wondered what was coming next.

The consultant spoke of my mother starting a course of radiotherapy and hormone therapy in addition. I thought he said it was a precaution to ensure that the cancer did not return, which sounded like a good idea to me.

'Oh,' my mother and I said in unison.

There was more, about appointments, the treatment and how it would make her feel. The main thing was a firm assurance that the prognosis was good, and statistics were quoted to support this.

Her life it seemed was back on track, her hopes for a long and happy future were firmly in place and I couldn't have been happier for her. Mine, however, despite recent revelations and changes, seemed still to be hanging in limbo. I knew I didn't want to return to my destructive habit of looking back instead of looking forward – I had spent too many years doing just that and it was definitely time to move on – but I didn't know where I was going or what I wanted to do with the rest of my life.

'Perhaps you *should* go back to Canada,' Lloyd suggested, his tone surprisingly gentle, 'spend time with your father's other family and lay a few ghosts. Before you start worrying, I can water your garden and take care of Ellie for you. She spends as much time with me as she does with you these days anyway, and she'll be quite safe with me.'

I knew we were both thinking of Adrian but he did finally seem to have got the message and I hadn't seen or heard from him in weeks. I hoped he would find someone new to be happy with in time – I just knew for sure it wasn't going to be me and I was equally sure that by now he knew that, too.

It was almost a relief to get away and this time my arrival in Victoria, British Columbia was very different. They were all there waiting at the airport to greet me as one of the family, all of them smiling. Cheryl, Julie, Jared and Ashlyn – the sister I had become so fond of in a surprisingly short time – who threw herself into my arms and hugged me so tight that I could hardly breath. I had absolutely no reservations about hugging her back, where once I would have held myself aloof and fought against such familiarity.

'Look at the pair of you together.' Cheryl beamed her pleasure. 'The likeness between you is unmistakeable, despite the difference in your colouring. This time I hope you will get the chance to enjoy your stay in the country that your father came to love so much.'

Once I would have come back with the rejoinder that he had chosen the country over and above his family in England, but now I accepted this was not exactly the case. It seemed strange to realize that Canada was once supposed to have been my home, too, and I made up my mind to look at it through different and more accepting eyes.

To Ashlyn's obvious disappointment, I chose to stay with Julie as I had done before. She had made me so welcome when I came as a stranger and I knew she would welcome my company. I also felt it was too much, too soon to be thrust into the bosom of my late father's replacement family – in particular how I would have felt living in such close proximity to Jared when I understood neither my feelings for him nor his for me.

Sitting in the late June sunshine and watching the hummingbirds fly to and fro, I pictured myself doing the same as a child. Would I have found the travelling between parents confusing or simply accepted it as a fact of life as children often do? It was something I would never know now and I still found it impossible not to feel just a little bitter that I had never been given a choice.

Looking through the box had been upsetting, because besides the letters and photos my father had received from my mother, he had added cards – one for each birthday and Christmas for every year of my life, one for my confirmation and one for my wedding day. It was heartbreaking to think he had never felt able to send them, and to realize that for much of my life he didn't even know where I lived – but then, I hardened my heart and reminded myself that was because he had made no effort to find out.

Sitting through the reading of the will I soon became aware that my father was quite a wealthy man and that no one else seemed surprised by this except me. The company was left to Jared; it was clear from the wording of the will that Mitch had looked upon him as the son he had never had. I might once have had a problem with this but I knew Jared better now and accepted he was more than deserving of the huge trust placed in him.

Both Cheryl and Ashlyn had been left extremely comfortably off and I was surprised and pleased to have been included with them and Julie in the allocation of a number of shares in the company. There were various other bequests and that, it seemed, was that.

There was a dry cough as we began to fuss with bags and jackets prior to leaving, and everyone paused to stare at the man still sitting behind his desk as he began to speak.

Both the words and the sum of money revealed made my head spin, especially as they alluded to me.

'No,' I said emphatically, suddenly on my feet and leaning towards the man with both hands flat on the desk, 'no, I don't want a penny of it.'

'I suggest,' the man said calmly, holding out a letter with my first name written across it in a bold black scrawl, 'that you read this before you come to any decision.'

I ended up with Jared – as I had done that other time – in his huge four-by-four high above the sea and we were arguing.

'What's the point?' I demanded. 'Whatever is in here,' I tapped the envelope on my lap with the tip of my fingernail, 'is too little, too damn late. Why didn't he write to me years ago when I might have been able to appreciate it?'

'If you read the letter,' he pointed out, 'you might find out.' He took me gently by the shoulders, looked into my eyes and reminded me, 'You let your mother have her say, Fran. The least you can do is to allow your father that courtesy, too.'

What could I say? I knew he was right – as he usually was, damn him.

Climbing down from the huge vehicle, I closed the door and standing on tiptoe, said, 'I won't go far. Will you wait for me?'

'I'll be right here.'

There were seats, a low stone wall, and blue sea stretched out as far as the eye could see, dotted by tiny islands. I sat and opened the envelope and the sun felt warm on my head as I slipped the letter out and began to read.

My dearest Francesca, my own darling daughter,

If you have received this letter then it is already too late for me to try to make amends for my absence from your life or to tell you of my love for you in person, and for that I can only say I am sorrier than you will ever know.

When I left you behind in England all those years ago it was to build us all a better future together overseas. I truly had no idea I was saying goodbye to you forever and when I discovered that you and your mother would not be joining me, it was already too late to turn the clock back. I had settled status and a new life here in Canada and you had your life in England.

I cannot and do not blame your mother for the decisions she made at the time because she made those decisions in good faith and I did understand her reasons to a certain extent. We were little more than strangers when we married and it's understandable that she didn't want to give up all that was familiar to join me halfway across the world. However, I should have tried harder to change her mind about allowing contact between you and I and for that I do blame myself. It is a regret I have lived with all my life and I have discovered over the years that regrets are worse than any mistake you could ever make.

I should also have made the effort to trace you when you were older, but it never seemed like quite the right time to burst into your life and introduce myself as your father. If you had made the decision not to make contact, which seemed likely, I felt it was not up to me to force the issue because I had no rights. I gave up those rights when I left – whatever the reason. I'm afraid I also always thought there was plenty of time.

Please don't feel that my love for my new family ever meant I loved you less because I never stopped loving you for a single minute, Francesca, and I never stopped missing you. Receiving the letters and photos was both a blessing – because they enabled me to hear about your progress and see that you grew more beautiful with the passing years – and a torment – because I should have been there to share in your joys and triumphs and to give you away as a bride.

I hope that you have had a good family life with your mother and your stepfather. I am sure he is a good man who loves you dearly, but I hope in a corner of your mind there has always been a place for the father who gave you life and would have given anything to share it.

Hindsight is a wonderful thing and it would be easy to say, looking back, that I might have done things differently, but we cannot change the past, only the future.

I haven't been the father to you that I imagined I would be on the day you were born. I haven't been there to take care of you for too many years of your life and I am all too aware the money I am leaving you after my death will never be able to make up for that. I just hope that you can accept it as a father's gift to a beloved daughter. I couldn't be there to share your youthful dreams but we're never too old to dream and I hope you might use some of my gift to you to make your dreams come true.

With love always,
Daddy

Running back to Jared in floods of tears, I found him standing beside the Hummer and fell into his arms. He held me while I cried my heart out, and it felt good – as if I was washing away all those years of hurt. Then we looked into each other's eyes and I knew he was going to kiss me. I lifted my face in eager anticipation but when his lips met mine I felt nothing – nothing at all – and I could see from his expression as we drew apart that it was the same for him.

The red-hot passion I had expected was nothing more than lukewarm fondness yet, far from being disappointed, I found I was actually relieved. We smiled and hugged accepting that this was how it was meant to be, with nothing more than friendship between us and the love one family member has for another. Jared was just as much my brother as he had been my father's son – in every way that counted. I knew I was happy with that. My life wasn't with Jared after all and it wasn't in Canada.

The slight crunch as the wheels hit the runway jolted me out of a reverie that had occupied my mind for almost the whole of the long flight back to England. The holiday was well and truly over but I was rested, settled in my mind and probably happier than I had ever been in my life before. The journey to the truth had been a long time overdue and now the rest was up to me.

I thought of my father's words and his wish that I should pursue my dreams and I even wondered if those vague dreams I'd once had of starting my own recruitment agency might be worth considering again. I'd always wanted to be my own boss and now that I was free of Adrian's interference there was nothing to stand in my way. The idea was exciting and the world was suddenly filled with possibilities.

Who knew what the future held? At least now what had gone before had been dealt with and responsibility for past mistakes accepted by my parents – and also by me – because I, too, could have made an effort and changed the course of events at any time in my adult life instead of just blaming others.

'Fran.'

I blinked, still bleary from the long flight. The sea of smiling faces around the barriers bobbed and weaved in front of my unsteady gaze and I gripped the handle of my trolley more firmly. I wasn't expecting anyone to meet me – no one knew which flight I was on, except …'

'Fran.' A firmer and rather larger hand than mine grasped the handle. 'It's good to have you home,' Lloyd said warmly, smiling down into my eyes, 'I've missed you.'

'Lloyd.' I didn't even try to hide my delight. 'I've missed you, too.'

Tall, tanned and rugged, solid and dependable, he was everything I never knew I wanted in a man and I stared up at him, shocked by a sudden surge of desire that seemed to come from nowhere.

I found it impossible to look away and we stood there staring at each other, grinning like imbeciles, suddenly unaware of all the people milling round us in the busy airport terminal. Then I was in Lloyd's arms and there was nothing lukewarm about a kiss that was filled with all the passion my deprived heart could ever have dreamed of.

I had travelled – twice – halfway around the world in my search for the truth, discovering my family and myself in the process. Love had not figured anywhere in my plans, but looking at Lloyd I found myself wondering if that old cliché still applied and home really was where the heart is. Could it be possible love had been there all along – literally right on my own doorstep?